HOT ZONE

-Major Crimes Unit-

by Iain Rob Wright

Hot Zone

Major Crimes Unit #2

ISBN-13: 978-1508842415
ISBN-10: 1508842418

Cover art by Stephen Bryant
Interior design by Iain Rob Wright

www.iainrobwright.com

Give feedback on the book at:
iain.robert.wright@hotmail.co.uk

Twitter: @iainrobwright

More Books by Iain Rob Wright

THE FINAL WINTER

ASBO

ANIMAL KINGDOM

SEA SICK

SAM

RAVAGE

SAVAGE

THE HOUSEMATES

SOFT TARGET

HOLES IN THE GROUND

THE PICTURE FRAME

2389

HOT ZONE

A-Z OF HORROR

NOTE FROM THE AUTHOR

Thanks for picking up book number 2 in the Major Crime Unit series. I hope that means you read book 1 (Soft Target) and enjoyed it. If not you can get it here. This latest adventure for Sarah Stone and the MCU gang was a lot of fun to write and focuses on some of the threats that we face right now in the world, but please do not be afraid. This is just a work of fiction. You are quite safe. Before you begin, I just need to quickly tell you that I could not have written this book without the following two people.

Jack Millis – the greatest fan and friend a guy could ask for. He helped me with a lot of the character work and if my characters jump off the page, it's because of him.

Nev Murray – a great guy and a constant supporter of my work. He helped me whip this book into shape so that you can enjoy it. He runs a fantastic blog dedicated to reading at the following address. Check it out:

www.confessionsofareviewer.blogspot.co.uk

And without further ado, please turn the page, keep your hands inside the cart at all times, and get ready to take that plunge.

"Lord have mercy upon mankind. Deliver and save the world from the dreadful Ebola Virus."

– Lailah Gifty Akita

"It's one billionth our size and it's beating us."

– Sam Daniels, Outbreak (1995), Warner Bros."

-0-

"Dr Krenshaw, are you busy? Mrs Drayton hasn't been seen in almost two hours and she's becoming difficult. Could you spare a minute to see her?"

Dr Alistair Krenshaw, an epidemiologist by specialisation, but willing to help out however he could, noticed the young brunette and smiled. Not even thirty-years-old, he suspected, and an attractive young thing for sure, yet he couldn't, for the life of him, remember her name.

"Of course," he said. "Would you like to fill me in on her condition, Nurse...? I'm sorry, you seem to have forgotten your name badge."

The nurse looked down at the bare patch on her tunic and blushed. "Oh, no, I had it earlier, but one of the patients on the night shift got a little...grabby. I must have lost it then. My name is Suzanne."

"My word, are you okay, Suzanne?"

"Nothing I'm not used to at 3AM on a Friday night, Doctor."

Krenshaw patted Suzanne softly on the shoulder, admiring her ability to deflect an incident others might have made into an issue. "So," he said, "what seems to be the problem with Mrs Drayton?"

"She's been complaining of stomach cramps, can't keep anything down. We have her on a drip, but she's demanding that we give her something for the pain. It's a simple case of gastroenteritis but she's making a meal of it. We really need to free up her bed, though. We're inundated with new admissions since they closed St Elizabeth. These spending cuts are going to put us all in early graves."

Krenshaw knew patients like Mrs Drayton well. Most patients were subservient, looking upon doctors with complete reverence, while those like Mrs Drayton thought they knew exactly what was wrong with them and exactly how they should be treated. Gastric conditions made patients feel like their lives were hurtling to a painful end, but it would always pass within 24 hours or so; trying to make someone with stomach-flu understand that was always a challenge.

Doctor and nurse entered the A&E ward and visited Mrs Drayton in her cubicle. Lying on the bed, the old woman was a picture of misery, with grey hair matted against her sweating forehead and horn rimmed spectacles as crooked as her nose.

"Are you the doctor?" Mrs Drayton demanded, before clutching her stomach and moaning.

Krenshaw smiled without warmth of any kind. It was a skill he had learned, just as he had learned how to take blood and administer a suppository. "I am a consultant," he explained, "but your nurse, Suzanne, summoned me to come speak with you. I understand you are in some discomfort."

"I'm on death's door," the woman said, clutching her stomach again. "I need summin' for the pain."

"I suspect you have a virus, Mrs Drayton. Uncomfortable and painful it may be, but very little that can be done about it unfortunately, other than allowing it to run its course."

The old woman's face puckered, not from pain but anger. "Bleedin' NHS. Useless. You don't wanna help nobody. I had to wait twenny-minutes for an ambulance because you lot closed the St Elizabeth. It's all about saving money for your fat bonuses, ain't it?"

Krenshaw glanced at the comely Nurse Suzanne, who was rolling her eyes and huffing. He gave the girl a subtle grin before turning back to the disgruntled patient. "Okay, Mrs Drayton. If you insist you cannot cope with the pain, we will do what we can." He plucked out his prescription pad, scribbled something on it, and handed it to Suzanne. "Nurse, could you fill this for Mrs Drayton and get her some pain relief, please? I will take a brief look at her charts while you're gone. Anything I can do to earn that fat bonus, no?"

"Of course, Doctor." Suzanne left the cubicle.

"Thank you, Doctor," said Mrs Drayton, sounding like a completely different person now she'd got her way. "I hate to be a bother, but I'm in absolute agony. I feel like I'm dyin'."

Krenshaw smiled at the patient, showing his teeth in something not far removed from a snarl. "Mrs Drayton, I have worked in places as far flung as the Congo, Sudan, and even Malaysia. I have seen men and women bleed from their eyeballs and cough up tissue from their lungs. I have seen the destruction wrought by evils such as Ebola, HIV, and Dengue Fever. What you have, Mrs Drayton, is a tummy bug. Now, I have sworn an oath to help you and help you I will, but please refrain from the hyperbole because it hurts my ears."

Mrs Drayton looked at him like he'd just broken wind, so revolted was the expression on her face. For a moment she merely trembled, but then finally exploded. "How dare you speak to me that way. I pay your wages. Bleedin' NHS. Where do they get you people from? I remember when doctors used to have manners. The way you just spoke to me is disgusting."

Krenshaw ceased paying attention to the vitriolic harridan and instead checked upon her readings. All of Mrs Drayton's vitals were fine, as expected. Her salt levels had come back low, but the saline drip would remedy that. He went over to the drip stand and examined the contents. The saline bag was full, recently changed by the lovely Nurse Suzanne.

With his back still to the ranting Mrs Drayton, Krenshaw reached in and removed something from the breast pocket of his doctor's coat. The ampule was attached to a syringe he had fashioned himself and filled with a liquid he had brought all the way from Liberia several years before. He had been keeping it for just such an occasion. Removing the barrier from the needle's tip, Krenshaw pierced the top of the saline bag just above the fill-line, then pressed down gently on the syringe, not needing to use much of the contents to get the desired result. Mrs Drayton continued howling indignities at his back, oblivious to the fact he was killing her.

Suzanne returned just as he was recapping the syringe and plopping it back inside his breast pocket. He gave her a quizzical look. "That was quick."

She smiled, but it became more of a smirk. "I didn't want Mrs Drayton to be in pain any longer."

Mrs Drayton noticed Suzanne had returned and so changed the focus of her tirade. "Give me them blasted pills and lemme out of 'ere, right now. I can't believe the way your colleague just spoke to me. I'm gunna lodge a serious complaint, you just see if I don't. Disgusting. You should both be sacked. Bleedin' NHS."

Krenshaw stepped out of the cubicle and waited for the nurse to finish her duties and follow him. When Suzanne eventually stepped out to join him, he raised a dark eyebrow and chuckled.

"I believe I've freed up that bed for you, Nurse. That is, unless you've persuaded Mrs Drayton to prolong her stay."

Suzanne tilted her head as she looked at him strangely. "Whatever did you say to her?"

"Nothing that was not true." Krenshaw told her. "When does your shift end, Nurse?"

"In an hour. Do you need me to do something?"

"Only come have breakfast with me. It's been a wretched night shift, wouldn't you agree?"

Suzanne blushed. Ten years younger than Krenshaw, at least, but he had seen the attraction every time she looked at him. Eventually she managed to answer. "I would love to, Doctor."

"Excellent. And, please, call me Alistair."

"Okay... Alistair. I will meet you out front in an hour."

"I look forward to it. I will carry on with my rounds until then. You know how it is: always more people to treat." He patted the ampule of liquid in his breast pocket and began to laugh.

Nurse Suzanne did not understand the joke. She would soon.

-2-

Howard was alone when he arrived at Reading's Whiteknight Hospital. It was a hive of activity, more so than normal for a hospital. Doctors and nurses buzzed around inside as well as out, and a great white tent had been established in the grounds. A cadre of police officers kept back anyone without proper business in a way that made the place seem more like a crime scene than a centre of healing.

Howard pulled into the parking lot and headed towards a cordoned area reserved for officials. He flashed his badge at the attending steward and pulled up beside a shiny red Audi. The steward came over and greeted Howard as he got out of his car.

"The quarantine has been set up on the lawns," he said, "but the response team is operating inside the hospital. There's a triage operating in the A&E and you'll probably find someone in charge there." A brief silence ensued while the steward stared at Howard with a strange grin on his face. Then the man said, "So they've called the MCU in on this, have they? Congratulations on saving the Queen last year. I saw it all on the news."

Howard nodded. "Thanks."

He didn't have time for conversation, so he politely dismissed the steward and headed off towards the hospital. The walk was short, thanks to the prioritised parking, but the closer Howard got the slower he walked. Something about hospitals scared him far worse than any member of Al-Qaeda or deranged lunatic. Disease tore a man apart secretly from the inside and waged war with no other agenda than to win.

When Howard passed by the monolithic tent on the hospital's lawn, he took a quick glance at the entrance flap. The men and women inside the tent all wore white 'spacesuits,' which made them look more alien than human. Their appearance was enough to send another wave of panic through him, as it likely did any other member of the public, which was why none of the space suited personnel lingered outside the privacy of the giant tent for more than a handful of seconds. Nor had anyone in authority yet spoken the word, Ebola. As much as the media was trying to incite fear, the government was trying to play things down. Howard knew the truth, though; that over four hundred cases of Ebola had been reported and that over two-thirds of them were currently at Whiteknight hospital being treated. Somehow the bogeyman of West Africa had made its way to the United Kingdom, and had done so with vigour.

Wanting to find someone in charge, Howard headed towards the A&E entrance, stepping around the back of an ambulance with flashing lights and passing through the open glass doors. Chaos reigned inside. The hallways teemed with the sick and injured, while nary a nurse or doctor remained in sight. With the major health crisis confined to the tent outside on the lawn, only a skeleton crew remained inside the hospital proper, and that didn't help the old man moaning on an unattended gurney or the young man with his nose dripping blood down his shirt. The injured and infirm stumbled around like zombies, seeking help from whoever would listen.

Howard managed to flag down a solitary nurse. She hurried over to him, but seemed like she had a hundred other places to be.

"May I help you?" she asked wearily. Her name badge read: Suzanne.

"Hello, Suzanne. I'm with the MCU. I need to speak to whoever is in charge of the quarantine outside."

"They're set up in maternity ward 1. You want Mr Cotta."

"Thank you." Howard hurried away, eager to exit the pandemonium of the A&E ward. He left the atmosphere of coughs, sniffles, and moans, and entered into the eerie silence of the maternity ward. The large space was mostly empty except for the rear of the ward where a dozen beds would typically be lined up, but were now probably being used inside the big white tent. Now the ward contained only a single, long desk with a large projector screen set up at one end and a dozen chairs around it. A handful of men and women looked over at Howard as he entered.

"May I help you?" Howard was asked for the second time in as many minutes.

"I'm Agent Howard Hopkins of the MCU. I'm here to investigate the possible terrorist implications of this current health crisis. I believe you are expecting me."

"Indeed we are," said a middle aged woman in a doctor's coat. She trotted over to him and offered her hand. "My name is Doctor Hart. I'm the hospital's senior pathologist. Mr Cotta here is in charge. He's been loaned to us by the World Health Organisation."

A tall, razor-cheeked gentleman with hard grey eyes nodded and spoke in what, to Howard's ears at least, sounded like an Italian accent. "Pleased to meet you, Agent Hopkins. I am afraid our most pressing concern is treating and containing this outbreak, not helping law enforcement find out what caused it. Surely that can come afterwards?"

Howard saw the awkward expressions on everyone's faces and realised that Mr Cotta was no friend to anybody there. He was a problem solver, sent in to take charge; similar to Howard in some respects. "I understand your priorities perfectly well, Mr Cotta. They are not dissimilar to my own. If terrorism is responsible, there could be further outbreaks. Therefore, finding those responsible is the best way of keeping this situation contained, wouldn't you agree?"

Mr Cotta stared at Howard for a moment, statuesque in his stillness. Then he spoke, "Very well, Agent Hopkins, you may have a seat at the table, but please do not impede our work."

"The last thing I wish to do, as I am sure you would not wish to impede mine." Howard took a seat, despite everyone else electing to stand. It would make it easier for them to forget he was there.

"I don't understand how the outbreak is so staggered," one of the doctors said. "The most mature cases are almost three weeks old, the newest less than one week. If the virus had spread organically then it would have been more systematic. This is almost like a dozen outbreaks spread out over time."

"As if someone were infecting people purposefully?" asked Howard.

Dr Hart nodded affirmatively. Her hair was quite strikingly blonde. "Quite possibly. If somebody has a strain of Ebola virus they could potentially infect people by injecting them or finding some other way of compromising their system. Typical infection is through contact with bodily fluids but a pure form of the virus would be even easier to catch."

Howard leant an elbow on the table. "Has anybody asked the patients whether they came into contact with syringes recently? We need to canvass them for common similarities."

"It's very hard to quiz somebody suffering with Ebola," said Cotta. "What with all the agony and dying they are doing. Do you see?"

Howard frowned. "I thought Ebola was relatively treatable in the early stages."

"Perhaps you are thinking of rabies, Agent Hopkins."

"It's not so," explained Dr Hart. "There is little we can do for Ebola sufferers other than keep them hydrated and try to steer them through. The death rate for Ebola in areas with good health care is usually around 40%, but this current outbreak has been far worse. We have lost more than 70% of the initial victims. It appears the traditional ebolavirus we are used to seeing has mutated, possibly tampered with."

"We are calling it Ebola Reading," said Cotta. "There were previously five different species of ebolavirus, only four known to affect humans. This is the sixth."

Howard felt his stomach juices crash against his insides. "How is this species of the virus different?"

"It is just worse," said Cotta bluntly. "Perhaps you should go and see for yourself, Agent Hopkins. Trust me, it will intensify your efforts to stop this virus from spreading."

"I'll take you," said Dr Hart. "Mr Cotta is right. If you are involved in stopping the outbreak, then you should see it first-hand."

Howard wanted to get out of his chair and run screaming to an isolated cave where nobody could ever so much as sneeze near him, but he was an agent of the Major Crimes Unit and his job was to find out who was behind the Ebola outbreak and bring them to justice. His fear was secondary to the task at hand, so he got up gingerly from his seat and nodded. "Thank you, Dr Hart. Let's get it out of the way so we can get back to business."

Cotta snickered. "Try not to look so unwell, agent Hopkins. It would be embarrassing if you were to faint."

***

As soon as Dr Hart signed Howard into the entry register and led him inside the giant white tent, he was grabbed by a gang of chaperones and bundled into one of the spacesuits. They taped up his wrists, sprayed him with a fine mist of something he imagined to be bleach, and went through the safety protocols with him.

"Do not touch the patients. Do not touch any bodily fluids of the patient. If you do come into contact with bodily fluids, remain where you are and alert your nearest colleague. Do not remove your safety equipment. If your safety equipment develops a tear or rip, remain where you are and alert your nearest colleague. Dispose of all needles and sharps in puncture-proof sealed containers. When you wish to exit the quarantine area, you must do so through the decontamination area and wait for clearance."

"It's not as scary as it sounds," came Dr Hart's voice inside Howard's helmet. The slight crackling nature of it let him know that there was a cheap radio system installed into the suits.

"Really?" he said back. "Because this is about as nervous as I've ever been – and I've been shot by a serial killer before."

"Ebola is harder to catch than you think. Most people who have caught it in the past, mostly in the 3rd World, have been friends, relatives, and health care workers in regular, prolonged contact with the infected. You are quite safe inside your suit."

"How is this thing spreading if it's not easy to catch?"

"That's what I thought you were here to find out, Agent Hopkins. It shouldn't be so easy to catch, which is why your concerns about terrorism hold water. If somebody is responsible for what you are about to see, then I hope you catch them and throw them in a very dark cell."

Dr Hart led Howard through a plastic flap and into the first section of the vast tent. Each bed was partitioned from the next by a curtain and there were even portable toilets with pull-around privacy drapes. The people here looked more terrified than ill. They had puffy eyes, sweaty foreheads, and didn't seem entirely comfortable in their beds, but most of them seemed okay for the most part. One woman was even reading a trashy magazine and chuckling to herself periodically. The front cover held the headline: Tom Cruise Worships Aliens, followed by the smaller byline of: Meet the Zombie Boy Who Likes Turtles.

"The early stages resemble influenza," Dr Hart explained through the radio. Fever, headaches, joint and muscle pain. Patients are bedridden and weak, but they are able to cope. Some extremely rare cases get better after this stage. They are the lucky ones."

Howard glanced at the woman with the magazine and wondered if she was one of the 'lucky ones.' Then he decided that no one with Ebola was 'lucky,' even if they got well. Dr Hart led him over to the next flap of plastic, which sectioned off the next area.

"Are you ready?" she asked him. "We are about to see patient's in the later stages of the disease. It will be distressing."

Howard took a few deep breaths, embarrassed when he realised that they would be echoing though the radio in Dr Hart's suit. "Okay," he said. "I'm ready."

They passed beneath the flap into the next room. This area took up the majority of the tent and was approximately the size of a narrow football field. Rows upon rows of beds were filled with the sickest people Howard had ever seen. A teenaged girl to his left lay beneath bloodstained sheets, a trickle of blood leaking from her ear and staining the pillow. Her entire face had gone an angry shade of purple and there was no expression on it other than pain and delirium. Another woman, a decade older, lay trembling and muttering as fever took her senses. From elsewhere in the room, a person wretched and vomited in the most painful-sounding fashion. Tears filled Howard's eyes.

It was like standing in the pits of hell, agony and fear intoxicating the very air itself. A dozen spacesuits milled about casually, unable to do anything but provide comfort and care. They were more caretakers of the dead than curers of the sick.

The teenaged girl spotted Howard standing at the foot of her bed and reached out a frail arm to him. She tried to speak, but all that came from her lips was a gargled choke followed by spitting blood. She slumped back on her pillows, eyes staring at the ceiling. An alarm sounded. Two spacesuits came rushing over, while a third pulled over a crash cart and started uncoiling a defibrillator.

"I want to leave," said Howard.

Dr Hart didn't argue. "Okay."

The three spacesuits started giving the young girl electric shocks, trying to jumpstart her heart. Her body leapt from the bed each time.

"Get me the hell out of here now," shouted Howard. "I need to leave. I need... I need... I can't breathe."

Dr Hart grabbed Howard by the helmet and pulled his visor up against her own. Through the plastic windows they made eye contact. "You're panicking," she said. "That's okay. Everybody panics. Just concentrate on your breathing and remind yourself that you are healthy. You are okay. You are not infected. These people are dying, though, and they need our help. We are going to help them. We are going to walk out of this tent and find a way to stop this. Okay?"

Howard couldn't nod because she still held his helmet, so he said, "Okay. I'm okay. I'm okay."

"Good. Follow me."

Dr Hart took him to the decontamination area where they showered in their suits before once again getting sprayed with the fine mist of bleach. Then they passed through into another area where they removed the suits and washed their hands, face, and necks thoroughly beneath scolding showers. They were then signed out and back in the fresh air a minute later. Howard took the longest breaths of his life.

Dr Hart patted him on the back. "Are you okay, Agent Hopkins?"

Howard managed to straighten up. "You just saw me almost wet myself. I think you can start calling me Howard."

"Then you can call me Stevie."

"Stevie?"

"Stephanie," she explained. "But my friends call me Stevie."

"Okay, Stevie. Thank you for keeping me calm back there. Please don't tell Mr Cotta. I think he knew this would happen."

"I won't mention it, and it's nothing to be embarrassed about. There's something instinctively terrifying about diseases. They send our inner caveman into a tizzy."

Howard frowned. "A tizzy?"

"That's about the best way to explain it. We're biologically conditioned to fear disease in the same way we would fear swimming with a crocodile. Our fear responses kick in and make us panic. It takes a while to overcome that. No reason to be embarrassed, I assure you."

"You're kind," Howard told her. "And brave."

"Ha! A member of the MCU calling me brave. I couldn't do what you people do. The way you stopped that terrorist last year. Were you involved in that, by the way?"

Howard thought about the events Stevie was referring to and nodded his head slowly. "I was involved, yes, but the real hero was a woman who was working with me. She was only with the MCU temporarily but was as brave as you are."

"Perhaps you should invite her back then."

"Yeah," said Howard, thinking: If only anyone knew where she was.

-3-

Sarah got out of bed and switched on the television, switching to the news as she always did this time in the morning. The old flat screen flickered persistently and the colours were odd at the corners, but it got her through the endless days. At first she'd hoped to see news of her imminent rescue, but other than some early reports of her initial disappearance, there had been nothing. The world did not seem to care very much that Sarah Stone was gone from the world. Her scarred, mangled face would not be missed, nor perhaps even remembered.

For a while, she had almost been able to conjure up the face of the man who had abducted her. The glaring eyes and straight teeth were a fuzzy image at the back of her mind, but it wasn't clear enough to make an ID. The blow to her head had cleaned her clock and wiped any memories she had of the events away.

Now she sat on her bed, staring at a familiar face onscreen.

MCU Director Palu seemed to have aged in the last year. The hair on either side of his head had gone a frosty white and he'd grown a moustache of the same colour. His medium-brown skin seemed a little paler too. Yet, when the man spoke he demanded authority, each word as confident as the last.

"The current outbreak has indeed been attributed to Ebola Virus," said Palu to a microphone, "as the press has indeed been speculating for days. The majority of cases have been contained to a temporary treatment site at Reading's Whiteknight Hospital. Everything that can be done for the patients and their families is being done. Everything that can be done to contain the current outbreak is being done. Everything that can be done to find a vaccine is being done. We, as yet, do not know what allowed this disease to enter our shores, but we have no reason at all to believe it will expand beyond our control. The National Health Service is doing all that it can to educate people on preventative measures and are confident that they can deal with the additional strain on resources this outbreak has caused. Thank you." He took no questions.

The news report switched back to the studio where the grim face of news anchor Jack Millis filled the screen. Sarah recognised the man, knew he'd made his name by reporting on the Dartmouth bombing she herself had been involved with. Now, Jack Millis spoke in the foreboding tones of a man who loved to make a crisis worse. The more people were afraid, the more they would look to him for guidance. How, Sarah would like to give the simpering fool a good hard kick in the nuts.

"A message of hope," he said. "Yet one has to ask themselves why the director of the MCU is involved in this crisis at all. Isn't the domain of the MCU terrorism and serious crime? Is their involvement a "sign" that this outbreak may not be the work of unfortunate happenstance, but instead the maniacal plotting of a deranged criminal? If terrorism is indeed behind this outbreak of one of the most deadly of diseases, then should we be preparing ourselves for further attacks, further outbreaks? Sobering thoughts, Britain. Sobering indeed. Thank you for joining me this morning. I'm Jack Millis and you've been watching Morning with JM."

Sarah grunted, switched off the television, and remained sitting on the bed. The MCU had been on the brink of closure when she'd helped them catch a terrorist named Hesbani. Now the organisation seemed to be going from strength to strength, and even expanding beyond the scope of terrorism. Last week she had seen on the news that the MCU had helped to apprehend an escaped serial killer, Richard Heinz. It appeared they were going from success to success, and she was glad. She looked back on her time with the MCU fondly, despite not doing so at the time. She'd been a broken mess when MCU agent, Howard Hopkins, had come to ask for her help. By the end of her association with MCU she'd actually started to look towards the future. Things didn't seem quite so bleak. Aside from the ones on the left side of her face, her scars had finally begun to heal.

Then someone had abducted her and any thoughts of the future became muddy and dark. She didn't even know if her captors intended to let her live, yet four months they had held her hostage without so much as questioning her. She'd been treated well and never tortured, yet any attempt she made to leave was met with immediate force. She hadn't been able to walk for a week the last time she'd attempted to attack one of her guards, so she had relented and resigned herself to her fate, watching the news each day to try and see if she could gain any clue into who was keeping her and if anybody was looking for her.

Her initial suspicion was that Hesbani's men were taking revenge on her for her interference in the terrorist plot last year, but they were savages who would want her blood. They would have tortured and beaten her, before executing her to provide a message to those who interfered with their agendas. Hesbani's supporters, however, had not even appeared in the news once. The man's operations had died with him; and his former boss, Al Al-Sharir, had not been heard from in almost a decade. The Shab Bakhair cell was finished.

So who the hell was keeping her and what did they want?

The door to her en suite room — for it was no cell by anyone's standards — opened and in stepped one of her regular guards. The short, stubby man was named Rat by his colleagues and he had likely got the name from his two sharp front teeth. He was friendly enough, yet there was no mistaking the violent nature of the man bubbling away beneath the surface. Sarah recognised it because she was the same. Yet, in her current predicament, her violent impulses were shackled and impotent. She had no outlet for her anger other than by trying once again to escape, but her body had not yet recovered from the last time.

Trying to figure a way out consumed most of Sarah's day, as it should have. A prisoner had a duty to think about attaining freedom and she was no different. While she suspected she might die soon, she also knew that she would do all she could to try and avoid that happening. Her next escape attempt would be her seventh and she hoped against hope that it would be the last.

"Brought you breakfast, sweetheart" said Rat, wrinkling his nose at her like the creature he was named after.

Sarah glanced at the watch they had let her keep and frowned. "It's almost afternoon."

Rat placed the tray of cereal and coffee on the bedside table and shrugged. "The lads were up late last night with business. We have other priorities than looking after you."

"I thought I heard something last night. What were you up to? Kidnapping children, or just molesting them?"

Rat didn't get angry. He was too used to Sarah's attempts to rile him. Instead he just flashed his rodent smile at her. "Only molesting that'll get done is on you if you don't keep a lid on that smart mouth."

"You'd need to find a dick first. I get the impression you're sadly lacking."

Rat chuckled. "When are you going to give up the attitude? I'll never take anything you say personally, so stop trying to get a rise out of me. You're my prisoner and have cause to hate me, so why would I be offended to find out that you do?"

"A very coherent statement for a degenerate like you, Rat."

"You'd be surprised how smart degenerates can be. In fact this country is run by degenerates, and where would we be without them?"

Sarah rolled her eyes. "Oh, here we go. Country of infidels and degenerates, huh? You're going to destroy us for the glory of Allah?"

"I don't fight for Allah, luv. Don't even like the fella."

"Then whom?"

"Certainly not for no god."

"Then what are you keeping me for? What agenda do you have?"

"I have no agenda. I take orders. Orders are simpler than agendas. They pay better, too."

Sarah was beginning to unravel the man without him knowing it. After months of getting nothing but silent treatment from Rat, she had got him to open up and start bantering insults with her. Now he had forgotten himself enough that he was dropping information without even realising it."

"You're a mercenary," she spat. "At least I can respect a fundamentalist. At least they're fighting for something worthier than money. They have a cause."

Rat back snapped at her. "I have a cause."

"To get rich? How very honourable."

"No, not just to get rich. I'm going to change things, make things better. I'm going to liberate the people of this country from the oppression of an unfair system."

"Sure you're not the first terrorist to think his cause is noble. You're misguided, same as the rest of them."

Rat let his calm slip a little and snarled at her. "I'm not a terrorist. I'm fighting for this country not against it."

Sarah eyeballed the man closely. "You're fighting for this country? How?"

"Just shut your goddamn mouth or I'll break your jaw again."

Sarah still felt the pain of the last beating, so decided to keep quiet. Rat might think himself a freedom fighter or hero of some kind, but he was not averse to giving a woman — and a prisoner no less — a good kicking. He left her room and locked the door behind him, leaving Sarah alone once again. She got off the bed and went over to the television. Her captors had screwed the set down onto the cabinet, but they had paid no mind to the back of television, where she had removed six delicate screws from the rear panel using the steel clasp of her watch. She was now able to slide the back off the unit with ease, and inside was her ticket to freedom.

The television's various circuit boards were pressed from copper, extremely sharp at the edges. Sarah had spent enough time examining the different pieces of electronics to understand that the PCBs were the closest thing she would find to a weapon. There was one attached to the television's inputs that was slim and about fifteen centimetres long, similar in size to the rulers children kept inside their pencil cases. She'd already unscrewed the PCB ahead of time, but had left it connected for the time being. Yanking it free would eliminate her use of the television for good, the only solace in her confinement, but it was the only thing she had managed to find in four months of confinement that was sharp enough to cut a man's throat.

She yanked the circuit board free and pulled out the wires, feeling its sharpness immediately. Its edges cut into her fingers as she clutched it tightly. She took it over to her bed and used a corner to slice a hole in her pillow case, and less than a minute later she had cut a strip of cotton and fashioned a makeshift grip around one end of the circuit board. Next she forced one of the sharp corners against the wall until it snapped, leaving behind a jagged, deadly edge. She did the same on the opposite corner and eventually managed to fashion a point. She had a knife. A flimsy, yet wickedly sharp copper knife.

All she needed to do now was wait for Rat's next visit.

-4-

Back in the makeshift office on maternity ward 1, Howard sat and listened to the experts once again. Currently, they were discussing the possibilities of what could have caused the outbreak of Ebola Reading. "It's very much the same virus," one of the doctors explained, pointing out a squiggly, knotted, worm-like creature on the projector screen. "The proteins are unaltered. The only changes seem to be within the binding cells, impacting the rate of infection on the host. If the virus has been tampered with, it has been tweaked in only a minor way, but even doing that much would take a genius-level knowledge of genetics."

"Is it possible that the virus changed on its own?" asked Howard.

"Absolutely," said Cotta. "Viruses mutate constantly to survive."

"Could it go airborne?"

Cotta shook his head. "Don't let the media fool you, Agent Hopkins. The Ebola Virus is too far removed from the ability to transmit that way. It would take millennia for an organism to evolve in such a way."

"But there's a possibility that the virus is being modified manually? Is it possible to make it airborne through engineering?"

Cotta shook his head again, even more adamantly. "It would be a profound achievement to even come close. If this is a case of genetic engineering, then I wholly suspect that this slight alteration is the sum total of whoever is responsible's ability. More important is how the virus got started. We need to find out why so many ex-patients of this hospital have come down with a rare 3rd World disease."

Howard sat forward and put his elbows on the table. "You just said ex-patients. What do you mean?"

Cotta looked at him and frowned. The man had a way of looking at the rest of the room like he were surrounded by children. "You don't know? Almost every patient in quarantine has visited this hospital within the last month or so. The first patients came in the longest time ago, several weeks. The newest cases were in this hospital as recently as 6 days ago. That is why all of the cases are local to the town of Reading. It seems that Whiteknight is the commonality in all these cases."

Howard chewed at the inside of his cheek. This was sounding more and more like something deliberate. "Then the source of infection is the hospital itself," he said.

Cotta nodded. "So it would appear."

Dr Hart added, "We have checked the blood bank, intravenous medicines, water supply, the cafeteria. All have been cleared of the virus. All in-patients have been relocated to the Royal Berkshire. We will be closing A&E within the next few hours and redirecting ambulances there as well. Then medical forensics will scour Whiteknight from top to bottom."

Howard pushed a strand of hair out of his eyes. "You said this thing passes via infected bodily fluids. Is there an area in the hospital that all the patients would have visited? An area where they may have all passed through?"

"We don't know," admitted Dr Hart. "There are many places where patients congregate, but the ones we have checked have been clear and there is one thing that doesn't fit about it being the hospital itself that is causing the infection."

Howard frowned. "Oh?"

"No employees of the hospital have been infected. Not a single one. Doctors, nurses, and porters are all healthy. It is only ex-patients who have been infected. If the reservoir was the cafeteria, for instance, then the infection rate would be the same amongst staff. There is nowhere that patients visit that staff do not."

"Which," said Cotta, "makes it highly likely that it is medical supplies or equipment that is at fault."

"Does this hospital have a strain of Ebola on site?" asked Howard.

Dr Hart shook her head. "Of course not. We have a pathology lab, but we use it only for testing patient samples. The nearest place that has Ebola on ice is probably Porton Down, and that's military."

"So how do you think this thing started?" Howard wasn't the expert here and he didn't intend to act like one. He was getting lost in the possibilities.

"We are checking the patient backgrounds," said Cotta. "Usually these things start after a patient travels to a 'hot zone,' a place where natural reservoirs of the virus exist. One of the early patients, deceased now, has family in Sierra Leone. Possibly he was the one who brought the Ebola Virus into the UK."

Howard nodded, but there were things that still did not add up. "That doesn't explain why this is a new strain, does it? Ebola Reading is different. People are dying in unnatural patterns. No doctors or nurses have been infected. Mother Nature is predictable, whereas man is quite the opposite. If this virus isn't conforming to typical behaviours, then it seems highly likely that someone is behind this."

Dr Hart agreed. "I don't doubt what you are saying, Agent Hopkins. The reason you are here is because there are certain elements of pre-meditation about this."

"We are not detectives," snapped Cotta. "We are here to study and contain the virus. We are wasting time trying to help agent Hopkins with his investigations. We have already dwelled on it far too long."

Howard didn't react. Cotta was making it more and more obvious that he resented MCU's involvement. Howard could even understand why. He was there to snoop and pry, to ask question after question, casting an ever wider net until he found answers. Cotta was concerned with exact opposite methods, working in ever decreasing circles until he had the virus trapped, understood, and contained.

"I would like nothing more than to get out of your way, Mr Cotta," said Howard, "but you experts, here, are the only ones who can answer my questions."

"I agree," said Cotta. "Which is why I will give you Dr Hart. Leave the rest of us in peace and direct your questions only to her from now on."

Howard looked at Dr Hart who seemed a little put out by her services being offered on her behalf but not upset or angry. She smiled at Howard and tucked a strand of blonde hair behind her ear. "Okay, I suppose that makes sense. Where would you like to begin?"

"With the staff. I want to know who saw to these patients."

Dr Hart frowned. "You think it was a healthcare worker?"

"I think somebody did this, somebody who knew what they were doing. A member of the public would be too ignorant of a virus like Ebola, not to mention incapable of getting a live strain of it. Anyone outside of the health industry would be terrified to be in the same room as Ebola Virus.

No, I think whoever did this was somebody comfortable being around deadly diseases. I think a doctor did this."

Cotta chuckled. "You have your theory, Lieutenant Columbo, now go investigate it somewhere else."

Howard smiled. "I will, but only after I interview everybody in this room."

***

Of course, Cotta had been furious at the indignity of having Howard disrupt his work, even though he himself was exempt from questioning. Cotta was from the WHO and had not even been in the country at the time of the initial outbreak. Several other members of his task force were also of no interest, for they had been loaned out from other institutions. Only a handful of the doctors and experts present worked at Whiteknight hospital fulltime and Howard gained very little from them to help his investigation. They all seemed like well-adjusted individuals, full of compassion and distress at the number of people sick on their watch. Howard took as much info as he could from them before deciding to take his investigation elsewhere — much to the delight of Cotta.

Dr Hart led him to a secure office that was piled with stacks and stacks of files and paperwork. "These are all of the patient records for the infected patients," she said. "Cotta has had them all placed into a digital database, but we'll have to do things the old fashioned way."

Howard moved over to the largest pile on the office's cheap pine desk and picked up the top file. "Sometimes it's easier to lay out the facts when you can hold them in your hands. Is there anything the patients have in common, other than having visited Whiteknight previously? They're all ex-patients, but what were they in for?"

"Absolutely everything," said Dr Hart, flapping her arms. "The first case was an old lady called Eleanor Drayton. She came in with a stomach bug but returned less than a week later with debilitating flu-like symptoms. We gave her a bed but didn't realise the severity of her condition until she started coughing up blood. The next cases came nonstop for days, ranging from people staying in the cancer wards to a group of outpatients who had only come in for minor procedures. One young man, who has thankfully shown signs of recuperation, came into A&E to have his pinkie reattached after cutting it off with a hedge trimmer. He went to surgery. There is no commonality, no department they all went to."

"Maybe they didn't go to the virus, maybe the virus came to them. Do doctors move around departments?"

"Not really. Some of the more senior doctors and consultants may have wide ranging expertise and help other departments when they are busy."

"Second opinions, you mean?"

Dr Hart nodded. "Or just picking up the slack for under-manned departments. Sometimes doctors may go on rounds, if they're free. It's something the directors of the trust promote in order to cut waiting times. If a heart surgeon is free, which is rare, granted, he might go down to A&E to deal with minor wounds, discharge those already seen to, or just fill in paperwork. It's not a popular scheme, especially with the more specialised doctors, but it has helped us rise slightly above our peers, which comes in handy when those same heart surgeons and oncologists want government hand-outs for expensive new equipment."

Howard opened up the folder in his hand and glanced at it. "Let's start at the beginning. Who dealt with Mrs Drayton?"

"Let me see," Dr Hart looked through the file for a few moments, checking over the squiggles and signatures that meant nothing to him. "Suzanne Mitchell was the attending nurse. Dr Chris Casey, the attending doctor. I know them well. Neither would have anything to do with this."

Howard said nothing, unwilling to rule anybody out.

"Wait, what's this?" Dr Hart pulled a handwritten page from the file and examined it. "It's a letter of complaint about Dr Krenshaw. He's an area consultant, one of the most senior doctors in the trust."

"Why did Mrs Drayton complain about him?"

"The usual. He was rude to her, allegedly. Krenshaw can be quite abrupt with patients. He spent a decade in Africa, treating AIDS, malaria..."

"Ebola?" Howard enquired.

"I don't know. He did a lot of humanitarian work, so I suppose he would have come up against it at some point. He is an epidemiologist with a PHD in infectious diseases."

Howard raised his eyebrow. "You mean the most qualified, most suspicious person in this hospital? Wow, you think you might have suggested his name earlier?"

"Look, Agent Hopkins. These are my colleagues, people I trust, people who have dedicated their lives to healing. While everybody might scream out 'guilty' to you, to me they are friends. I suspect none of them, but I am helping you because I know you have an investigation to do. Dr Krenshaw is a humanitarian, above reproach."

Howard gave no reply. He was verging on anger for not being informed immediately of Dr Krenshaw's suspect credentials immediately, but the longer the tense silence went on, the more he understood that Dr Hart and her colleagues were not conditioned to view each other with suspicion. They relied on one another too much.

"Okay," said Howard gently. "Where is Dr Krenshaw now? I need to speak with him."

"He isn't here. He moves between hospitals in the trust."

Howard folded his arms and thought. Did that make the man more or less suspect? There had been no confirmed outbreaks at other hospitals, so perhaps Krenshaw wasn't the source of the outbreak. There had also been no confirmed infections within the last few days — did that correspond with Krenshaw's absence?

"We need to cross-reference Krenshaw with the infected patients," Howard said.

Dr Hart exhaled and put her hands on her hips. "Okay, I'll get started."

Howard got started too. He leafed through a stack of files and was frustrated to find a dozen different doctor signatures. It seemed that no member of staff was exclusive to the infected patients, so that was his leading theory shot.

"I think I've found something," said Dr Hart.

Howard went over to the doctor where she sat cross-legged and barefoot on the floor. "What is it?"

"I've cross-checked the patient's original hospital visits — when they likely became infected — with the days Dr that Krenshaw was at Whiteknight. He was in the hospital the same times as every single patient infected with Ebola Virus. That might be true of other doctors, of course, but..."

"It certainly makes Krenshaw a person of interest, and with his specialisation in infectious diseases, I have to speak to him right away. Where can I find him?"

"I'll be right back," said Dr Hart, exiting suddenly and leaving her shoes behind.

Howard tapped his foot, anxious to get going. Everything added up to the culprit being this epidemiologist, Krenshaw, and if it was him, then the man could be planning another biological attack right that very second.

Dr Hart returned five minutes later, her lips thin, her nostrils flared. "I found out where Dr Krenshaw is," she said. "He's at Reading Children's Hospital."

Howard headed towards the door. "We need to move."

-5-

The door opened and Sarah readied herself. She was sitting on the bed, pretending to read a book she'd been given. Her heart was beating like a drum and she hoped the trepidation didn't show on her face.

It was Rat who finally entered, her most regular tormentor and the one she had expected to see. It was strange, but she had started to look forward to seeing his bucktoothed grin and dark, staring eyes. Rat's was the only face she saw for days at a time and it was sickeningly welcome against the loneliness and isolation she'd had to endure. But tonight, Sarah intended it to be the last time she was forced to look upon Rat's face with appreciation.

Rat was carrying a tray of what looked like Chinese food and it smelt delicious. Her captors would often bring her takeaway and snack foods rather than anything homemade. That suggested they were, at the very least, within a town or village, maybe even a city. If she were to escape, there would be places to go, people to plead to for help. She wouldn't need to get far, just out.

"I read that one," said Rat, pointing to her book. "The one where all the animals escape the zoo and attack people, yeah?"

Sarah eyed the cover of the novel and shrugged. "Only just started reading it. We can start a book club when I finish. You can bring the biscuits."

Rat smirked. "You haven't lost your wit, have you? Most people are morose by now."

"Most people don't know what the word 'morose' means. You're not as dumb as you look, which is pretty bloody dumb."

"As I've repeatedly told you, there's more to me than meets the eye."

"There's more teeth to you than meets the mouth."

That one seemed to hurt Rat a little. As much as he claimed indifference to her, he was starting to care. Stockholm syndrome worked both ways. As it was documented that hostages could start to enjoy the company of their captors, so too could captors begin to like the company of their wards. Rat was starting to think they were odd friends. She was about to wipe that foolish notion from his head.

"Who is keeping me captive, Rat? Tell me or I'll kill you." She made one last attempt to prise a name out of Rat and to give him a chance to do the right thing.

"Pope Francis," he replied dryly.

"Then you can tell the Pope that I gave you fair warning."

"Huh?"

Sarah leapt off the bed, sliding the shiv out from beneath her pillow and swinging it towards Rat's neck. His eyes opened wide as he realised what was happening. She'd caught him too far off guard for him to avoid the blade swiping through the air towards him. He snatched out at her but was wrong-footed and couldn't move fast enough.

He was going to die.

At the last moment, Sarah flinched and altered the direction of her swing.

She buried the shiv deep in the hollow beneath Rat's collarbone instead of her original target of his jugular. Much as she hated her captor, she couldn't say for sure that he deserved to die. His screams of agony did enough to satiate her need for revenge, but she was forced to wrestle with the man as he gritted his teeth and tried to grab her throat. Sarah grunted and strained, trying to fight the man off, but even wounded he was stronger.

"Bitch!"

Sarah growled. "Say that again."

"Bitch."

Sarah loosed rat's arm and grabbed the handle of the shiv, yanking it down like a lever. The wound opened up wider and Rat mewled like a kitten and slumped to the ground.

The shiv was narrow and thin, so came away easy as Sarah pulled it back from Rat's collarbone, leaving him to hiss and curse at her feebly. She stepped over him and headed to the unlocked door, the shiv dripping blood behind her. Before opening the door, she ran her hand over the blade and used the blood to cover her face. She would be up against dangerous men, and the best way to beat men in a fight was making them piss themselves before the first punch ever got thrown. A snarling woman covered in blood was enough to unnerve the bravest warrior.

Sarah left the room and entered a corridor. Despite the homely adornments of her incarceration, she now found herself inside the utilitarian hallways of some kind of factory or office building. It was the type of place where miserable employees marched around from nine-till-five. Currently it lay deserted. That boded well, for it meant her escape might not yet have announced itself. Rat's screams were loud, but they seemed to fade the further she went down the corridor. Around the next bend she was forced to stop.

A tough-looking guy with a shaved brown pate was leaning up against the wall and taking drags on a cigar. Against the backdrop of his black combat fatigues, the civilised gesture seemed out of place. Sarah smeared some more blood from her hands onto her face and put her theory into action. She staggered around the corner, hiding the shiv behind her back while glancing around erratically and chattering her teeth. The blood was still wet on her face.

"Paper pictures," she muttered. "Bits of string."

The confused guard threw his cigar down on the floor and stood on it, then just looked at Sarah. His dark complexion went almost white as he tried to comprehend what he was looking at.

Sarah made it even more confusing for him. She swung her one arm around like a jellyfish and hopped towards him. The other arm, with the shiv, she kept tucked behind her back. "The doctor in the house isn't dead," she muttered. "The teeth were not his."

"The hell is wrong with you? W-where's Rat?"

Sarah did a quick squat thrust then threw herself into the wall, bashing her forehead and kicking out like a wingless fly. "Boom goes the dynamite."

The guard seemed to realise that he had to do something. She wasn't just an insane woman, she was a prisoner on the loose. He stepped towards her and, as soon as he did, Sarah spun around and slashed his cheek with the shiv. As he recoiled, she booted him in the nuts and followed it up with a knee to the face as he doubled over. He was out cold.

Two down, Sarah told herself. How many more?

She raced down the corridor, passing through the only door at the end and hoping it led to salvation. When she opened it and passed through into what appeared to be a large warehouse, she was faced by a gang of glaring men. They seemed undeterred by the blood on her face and immediately sprinted towards her.

Sarah bolted left, heading for the nearest side of the warehouse that had windows. Maybe she could throw herself clear through the glass and get to safety.

The men chased after her, three of them in total.

There was a bench up ahead, piled high with what looked like engine parts. Sarah slipped past it, waving her arms and shoving a bunch of metal debris into the path of her pursuers. She heard a man curse as he no doubt stumbled over one of the obstacles, but all three men continued to chase her. As she got closer to the windows, she saw that she wouldn't be able to throw herself through the glass or scream for help. The frames started a good four-feet above the ground and did not lead outside; they merely separated one warehouse floor from the next.

There was nowhere to run.

Sarah spun around, swinging the bloody shiv.

"Put the blade down," one of the men growled at her, an older gentleman who had brought her food on occasion when Rat was busy, "and we'll be gentle."

"Or don't," said a younger man with bad skin. "And we'll make you fucking eat it."

Sarah wasn't going back to her room. She was done being a prisoner. They would have to beat her to death before she allowed them to recapture her. Perhaps four months in captivity should have tamed her like a canary, but it had only made her desperate like a trapped dog, and now she felt rabid.

"You can take me down," she said in a snarl, "but the first one to try loses an eye. Or a testicle. That's if you pussies have any."

A man she had not seen before, possessing a rough beard and scraggly grey ponytail, leapt for her then. She sent him back with a slice in his forehead the width of a pencil.

"Damn it!"

"Who's next?" Sarah waved the shiv menacingly.

Nobody else came at her.

She glanced around, trying to find an exit, but there were a dozen doors leading off from the warehouse and no telling where any of them led. Then she saw it. A fire exit. It seemed to sparkle at her like a beacon. If she could only reach it, if she could make it outside...

Sarah broke into a sprint, taking advantage of the men's reluctance to grab her and their surprise at her sudden bolt. They gave chase, but Sarah had bought herself enough of a head start to stay ahead of them. She raced across the warehouse toward the fire door, panting and moaning in excitement. The closer she got, the more certain she was that she was going to make it. She was going to escape. The men at her back were bellowing at her to stop, making her even more confident that she was going to get away. The rabbit was escaping the yapping dogs.

Sarah threw herself against the release bar of the fire exit and exited out into the glorious afternoon sunshine. She had hoped to find a street full of people, but instead found herself standing in a paved courtyard inhabited by a pair of black vans and a car she was sure she recognised. The sleek red Jaguar e-type caught her attention long enough to stop her in her tracks. It was a relic of her past.

From the corner of her vision Sarah saw someone step out behind her. When she turned around to face the stranger, something struck her hard beneath the chin. Her legs folded, vision tilted, and when she finally managed to see straight again, she was lying on the ground looking up at a face she knew well. A face she both loved and hated.

The stern green eyes glared down at her disapprovingly while Sarah shook her head in disbelief.

Only one word escaped her lips. "Daddy?"

-6-

"Daddy!" Sarah wanted to say other words but she couldn't. "Daddy..."

Her father looked down at her with an expression of irritation that had defined her childhood. "Most men manage to break out within three months," he said, "but then...you're not a man, are you?"

Sarah wanted to stand, but she couldn't move from her spot on the floor. "W-what?"

Her father offered his hand and yanked her up to her feet. "I'll explain everything, but get yourself cleaned up first. You look like a savage. I heard your scars were bad, but I had no idea they were so unsightly, especially with all that blood on your face. Come on, stop dawdling."

Sarah followed her father and allowed herself to be ushered back inside the warehouse, the place she had just fought so desperately to escape. Suddenly the torment of her four-month incarceration was forgotten and all that remained were burning questions. Had her father been keeping her locked up? Why?

She was directed to a toilet block and told to clean herself up and get the blood off her face. She did as she was told, feeling like a little girl, and came back out again as quickly as she could.

"I don't understand," she said as her father walked her to their next destination. The group of men who had chased her now strolled casually behind her. The grey haired man with the thick gouge across his forehead was chatting away merrily to one of his colleagues even as his face dripped blood. These were hard men, the type of men her father was used to working with. Major Stone was renowned throughout the British military as one of the SAS's most distinguished of distinguished men. He had seen action in every British conflict from the Iranian embassy siege right through to the most recent turmoil in Syria. He had spent a good portion of his life overseas or, at the very least, encamped somewhere ready to go overseas. Truth be told, Sarah barely knew the man.

A man staggered into the warehouse on the opposite side, getting everyone's attention. It was Rat, battered and bloody. He clutched the wound on his shoulder and walked in a stoop like Quasimodo. "Bitch stabbed me," he shouted, slumping over one of the floor's many tables.

Nobody seemed to care.

"Then perhaps you should have paid better attention," said Sarah's father flatly.

Rat said nothing else. He remained slumped in pain until his colleagues took him under the arms and led him away. That left Sarah alone with her father as they continued walking through the oily warehouse.

"Who are all these men," she asked him. "And what is this place?"

"They are my men, and this place is just an old assembly plant. I think they used to make elevator parts. What some men are willing to call a living baffles me."

"Don't you care that I stabbed one of your men?"

"Of course I care. Rat should've done better than to let you get the jump on him. I'll deal with him later."

"I meant, don't you care that he's injured?"

"He'll live, but I'm sure you intended that."

She nodded. "I don't kill a man unless I know he deserves it."

"Those feminine sensibilities will get you nowhere," he grunted. "The man was keeping you prisoner. He didn't deserve your mercy."

"He wasn't keeping me prisoner, you were. Why?"

"I'll get to that," he motioned towards an open office door and led her inside the dim, windowless room. She took a seat on one side of a gnarled wooden desk while her father sat on the other. One of his men appeared and handed him a glass of brandy before disappearing quickly. Sarah's father had not changed a bit in the years since she'd last seen him.

"Why am I here?" she demanded, regaining a slither of her courage now that she knew who was responsible for her capture. Despite her fear of her father, she no longer felt in danger. What harm could a man mean to his own daughter?

"Because you inserted yourself into things which did not concern you."

"What are you talking about? Why have you been keeping me prisoner? Why didn't you come see me yourself, instead of hiding behind Rat?"

"Because I needed to see how you operate under stress. I must say I am a little disappointed it took you so long to escape. Still, you are a woman, I suppose."

The comment from anybody else would have summoned Sarah's anger, but from her father it was crippling. "I thought I was going to die," she said meekly. "Is that what you wanted, me to be scared for my life? You're supposed to be my father."

"I am your father, and you are my daughter. I needed to see if you were capable of being anything more."

Sarah leant forward and placed her clenched fist on the table between them. She tried to maintain eye contact with her father but failed. She was twelve-years old again, pleading with him not to vanish for another year, but as much as she wanted to hate him right now, she did not want to make him mad, or make him disappear on her.

"I want answers," she said.

"Hesbani. There's your answer."

Sarah flopped back in her chair, both eyebrows raising of their own accord. "Hesbani? What about Hesbani?"

"You killed him."

Sarah said nothing. She wasn't sure what question to ask or what her father was getting at.

Her father accepted the silence as permission to continue. "Hesbani was my target. I had been tasked with bringing him home."

Sarah bolted forwards again. "You were helping a terrorist?"

"No, you stupid girl. I was helping the Pakistani government apprehend him. They wanted Hesbani for acts of terror he'd committed within their borders in protest against their cooperation with the British and American government. I had a man already embedded in Hesbani's operation, a man you knew..."

Sarah's eyes stretched wide as she realised. "Hamish?"

Her father nodded gravely. "A good man. Risked his life getting close to Hesbani. Pity you took him out."

"Only after her tried to take out me!"

Her father laughed, a rare gesture. "I admit he had issues, many of them aimed at you, but I wasn't very much interested at the time. Never did I think the two of you would cross paths. Regardless, Hamish is gone and so is Hesbani, along with my men's paycheque. Keeping you captive gave them some small restitution, but not enough by far."

Sarah shook her head in disbelief. "This was revenge?"

"Don't flatter yourself, Sarah. My men are not a bunch of simpering schoolgirls. We do not concern ourselves with things as petty as revenge. You have been held captive as a test. I wanted to see if you could escape. I was always against you joining the army, but you did it anyway and became a captain. I had resigned myself to almost accepting your bad decisions, especially when I heard you were unexpectedly married, but then the poor chap died, didn't he?"

Sarah thought about Thomas and almost let out a sob. She had gotten so good at not thinking about him that having him brought up unexpectedly got through her barriers and pricked at her heart.

"Then," her father went on, "you had your own accident and all but disappeared of the face of the earth. Licking your wounds, I assumed, but then, lo and behold, you pop up on the ten-o-clock news, hero of the hour. You even managed to make that ridiculous outfit, MCU, look respectable. Your victory saved them from the brink, you know? If you'd stayed on with them, I probably would've left you alone."

Sarah was still at a loss. Every couple of seconds she would remind herself that she was sitting in front of her father, the esteemed Major Stone, and would find it utterly surreal. Then she would remember that he had kidnapped her and held her hostage for four months and would get extremely angry. "Why didn't you leave me alone? You've been pretty good at that for most of my life."

Her father rolled his eyes. "Save the melodramatics. Some men are meant for more than raising ungrateful children into ungrateful adults. You have no idea the freedoms you have because of men like me. I have done more for you away then I ever would have at home. You had your mother, so don't act hard done by."

"Mum died when I was seventeen."

"Your childhood was already over, so why would you have needed her any longer? Anyway, I do not have you here to discuss family. You are here because you escaped, finally. As much as you interfering with Hesbani caused me great irritation, I was also impressed. It appears you do have a certain aptitude to our line of work, and to end up working within clandestine services, like your father, speaks of a certain family predilection, don't you agree? I wanted to see for myself how much of a man you are. You certainly wear your scars well. If you cut your hair short, I wouldn't even know you lacked a cock."

Sarah shifted in her seat. The thought of being anything like her father was akin to having bugs crawl beneath her skin. "Your men aren't SAS, are they?" she said. "They look more like mercenaries."

"And mercenaries is what they are. I am no longer in the employ of the British Army. I was tired of murdering civilians and bombing weddings based on the merest whiff of semi-accurate Intel. Do you know how many woman and children I have killed at the bequest of so-called Right Honourable gentlemen? One Prime Minister after another, sending hired thugs to murder and devastate their enemies, and for what? This woman we have in charge, Breslow, is worst of all. Her foreign war policy is going to double the amount of young men endangering their lives for worthless causes. All she cares about is getting her fingers in as many pies as she can. Thought people would have learned their lesson about putting women in charge with Thatcher. One thing I can assure you, sweet daughter of mine, is that no war I have ever fought in was waged for any other reason than to take what the other man has. I am a murderer, Sarah, I cannot change that, but I can change the reasons why. My days of taking orders from Westminster have stopped, and if I get my wish, I'll see the place crumble with Breslow buried beneath the rubble."

"So now you kill for money?" said Sarah, blinking. "Is that what you call honour?"

"It is more honourable to kill for money than the false flag of liberation. The British Empire hasn't liberated a single country in its entire existence — in fact it has only ever achieved the opposite. Now the Empire has crumbled and the Star Spangled Banner has replaced it with intentions even less noble and greedier. I am tired of the hypocrisy, Sarah. I fight for reasons of my own choosing now. As do my men."

"You didn't seem too concerned about Rat," she said. "You speak a good game, but you don't seem any more caring than you ever have."

"Rat is merely wounded. I do not weep for wounds. I am no woman."

"I don't know what you are, father. Tell you the truth, I'm tired of trying to figure it out. Am I allowed to leave here, or are you going to lock me back up?"

"You are free to leave," he said and she almost wept with joy. She kept her emotions contained, though, and gave only an imperceptible nod.

"Then I am going home." She got up out of her seat.

"You have no home, Sarah," Her father almost shouted it at her. "The Army did to you what it does to every soldier. It used you up and left you to die under the weight of your own nightmares. It sent you to war against people guilty of no crimes other than daring to have self-interest. Britain sends men like us to kill hundreds, in order to punish a scant few who actually deserve it. You, Sarah, are nothing more than a worn-down cog in a machine designed to trample poorer nations into the mud while blaming them for trying to claw their way out of it. Don't you want to do things on your own terms? Don't you ever wish you could put your skills, your experience, to a truly good cause?"

Sarah sat back down. "What are you talking about?"

"I am talking about recruiting you. A woman can be useful in certain situations and, as far as women go, you seem to be among the best."

"Better than most men," she grunted.

"Perhaps. I'm offering you a place on my team, Sarah. We fight for causes we believe in. We pay ourselves and fund our own operations. We do not take orders, we take jobs. If you are happy with your old life, daughter, then leave. Go back to whatever life you think you can have with that grotesque face of yours. Or join me and do what you're good at."

"And what is that?" she asked curiously.

"Killing bad guys."

-7-

Howard pulled the Range Rover up in a skid, leaving it in a disabled bay right outside the main doors of the hospital. His 'Official' plates would take care of any complainers.

"Where will we find Krenshaw?" he asked Dr Hart in the seat beside him.

"He oversees a training scheme for interns wanting to specialise in childhood diseases. His experience with the African orphanages makes him a key expert in the field. Many doctors have studied under him."

"Then I hope he is innocent," said Howard. "He sounds like a saint."

They headed through into the calm reception area and caught the attention of a receptionist, who seemed surprised then flustered by their urgency.

"C-Can I help you?"

Howard flashed his MCU badge. "Dr Krenshaw, where is he?"

The receptionist didn't need to check her computer. She knew off the top of her head. "He's on the 1st floor. Seminar Room 2."

Howard took Dr Hart by the arm and got her moving again. "I may need you to point him out to me. I don't want to announce my presence, in case he runs."

"This is crazy."

"I do crazy for a living," he said.

They took the stairs up, dodging past sick children still well enough to play ball in the corridors. Upstairs was quieter; deserted, in fact. From the signs on the walls and doors, it seemed that the 1st floor was dedicated to training and research. It had only one ward and that was a cancer ward. No doubt the sickest children were placed upstairs because it was more peaceful. Howard hoped that apprehending Krenshaw would be a calm affair. He was carrying a gun inside his jacket but had no intention of using it unless he had to, yet he followed protocol and unpopped the holster.

Dr Hart moved a little ahead of him and stopped just short of the door into Seminar Room 2. She turned to him and said, "You're not going to hurt anyone, are you?"

"I will do whatever the situation requires, Dr Hart. I understand you have divided loyalties here, but someone is responsible for infecting hundreds of people with Ebola. What do you expect to happen? If Krenshaw is our man, do you expect him to shrug and say, 'Oh dear, you caught me?' That's not how these things go."

Dr Hart looked like a sad kitten and Howard felt bad about being stern with her, yet he had a job to do and couldn't let her distract him. "You should stay here," he said. "I know I wanted you to point him out, but I would rather you out of the way unless necessary. There's no other way out of this room, is there?"

"I don't think so. I'll stay right here."

Howard approached the door and carefully opened it. Inside he found a small classroom of a dozen desks and twice as many seats filled with scribbling students. They all looked up at

Howard as he entered, but Howard's focus went to the front of the room where a large whiteboard lay unattended. The classic teaching position at the front of the classroom was unmanned.

"Where is Dr Krenshaw?" Howard asked the students.

A young brunette in spectacles answered his question. "He was unable to take the class today. He's helping the Paediatric Haematology department. It's on the ground floor."

Howard flew out of the classroom and grabbed a startled Dr Hart. "He's in the Haematology department. That's blood, right?"

Dr Hart nodded as they hurried. "Yes. This hospital specialises in malignant blood borne infections. They perform tests on children from all over the area to help study and diagnose Leukaemia and various lymphomas."

"I don't like the sound of this," said Howard.

"You don't think he's going to harm a bunch of children, do you?"

Howard took the stairs three at a time, shouting out to Dr Hart running behind him. "Whoever is behind the outbreak at Whiteknight is capable of doing anything."

"But Dr Krenshaw spent a decade helping children in Africa."

Howard saw the sign for MALIGNANT HAEMATOLOGY and headed in its direction. "I don't have the answers," he said. "Dr Krenshaw does and I intend to get them."

"You don't know he did anything. You don't know anything for sure."

Howard burst through the double doors at the end of the corridor and was met with the sight of a dozen sick children and their worried parents. Their heavy-lidded, dark-eyed stares made him shudder. Once again he felt like the very air itself was toxic and he forced himself to slow down.

"Are you okay?" Dr Hart asked him as he wobbled on his feet.

"I-I'm fine. I just...don't like hospitals. My father had three strokes before he died and my family seemed to be in and out of hospitals for years. I think it's the smell that brings back the memories."

Dr Hart nodded. "They're not meant to be fun places, but I'm sorry you had such a bad experience."

"Thank you. Let's get this over with."

Dr Hart pointed suddenly. "That's Dr Krenshaw, over there."

Howard followed her pointing finger to a tall, bony-faced man in a white doctor's coat. Krenshaw didn't see Howard marching towards him at first, but then he looked up from his clipboard and gave an expression of curiosity, followed by something else — was it concern?

"Dr Krenshaw?" asked Howard.

"Yes?" The man noticed Dr Hart standing beside Howard and nodded. "Stevie, always a pleasure to see you."

Dr Hart shuffled her feet and averted her eyes. "Thank you, Alistair. You too."

Howard took charge of the conversation, not wanting to give the doctor time to put his thoughts in order. "Dr Krenshaw, I am Agent Hopkins with MCU. Is there somewhere we can talk privately?"

Dr Krenshaw flashed a smile and said, "Of course, please, right this way."

He led Howard and Dr Hart though the ward towards a staff area at the back. All of the nurses seemed baffled by what was going on, but all of them smiled and nodded at Dr Krenshaw, obviously a man they liked and respected. Howard wavered momentarily from his certainty that Krenshaw was the man responsible for the outbreak. Perhaps he wasn't. All the same, questions needed answering.

"Just through here." Dr Krenshaw directed them.

Howard and Dr Hart moved past Krenshaw into a private office, but, as they did so, Krenshaw snatched out at Dr Hart and wrapped his arm around her throat, placing himself behind her. Howard spun around, ready to act, but stopped when he saw that Krenshaw had produced a syringe and placed it against Dr Hart's neck.

"HIV," Krenshaw stated calmly. "That is what is inside this syringe. Not quite as elegant as Ebola, granted, but just as incurable."

Dr Hart was frozen in unblinking terror. Her eyes were stretched wide and focused on Howard.

Howard backed off, kept his hands where everybody could see them. "Let's not do anything unnecessary, Doctor."

"Everything I have done is necessary."

"I don't understand. Explain it to me. Why Ebola? Why this?"

"Because people need to care." Krenshaw's lips moved into a snarl. "We cosy up in front of our televisions or sit on our air-conditioned trains listening to our iPods while half the world suffers in poverty. People in China toil in factories so that we can have cheap goods. Families in the Middle East live in dirt because any wealth their countries have either goes to us or the puppet governments we have left to rule over them. Africa is full of starving and sick children because we would rather spend our money growing fat and gluttonous than sharing with the 3rd World what we have. Maybe if the children of Britain start dying from Ebola, HIV, and malaria, we might just get down off our pedestals long enough to notice those begging at our feet. This country makes me sick. Now it is my turn to make it sick."

Howard nodded as if he understood, although he didn't. It was a worldview far too simplistic for him to accept "You're doing this to teach a lesson?"

"Yes. The only lesson this country will ever listen to. We are content to watch little black children and little Asian children dying on our television screens — it's no different to any other form of entertainment — but I wonder how indifferent this nation will be when it joins the 3rd World in its suffering and little white children begin to die. I'm sure it will be only too happy to fund all the cures the world needs then."

"I understand," said Howard. "It makes sense. I have seen the sick and the dying, too, thanks to what you have done, and I definitely see things differently now. Your plan has worked. I'm sure extra money is being spent on Ebola as we speak. You can stop all this. It doesn't need to go further."

Krenshaw shook his head with a grimace. "Eradicating Ebola won't even make a dent in the world's ills. There are a hundred more diseases that need attention, like the one inside this syringe."

Dr Hart spoke up, her voice aquiver. "Don't do this, Alistair. HIV is being cured. We're almost there."

"Then let me help speed things along."

Howard watched in horror as Krenshaw pumped the contents of the syringe into Dr Hart's neck, before shoving the wailing women away. The smart move would have been for Howard to leave Dr Hart and pursue Krenshaw, but rationality took no part in his decision as he wrapped his arms around the sobbing woman and helped her to the ground as she clawed desperately at her neck.

Krenshaw was out the door before Howard even had time to glance up. He didn't want to imagine what the murderous doctor would do next.

-8-

Sarah was sat eating a sandwich when her father came barging back into the office where he had left her to think. And think she had.

In a way her father seemed proud of her. She'd followed in his footsteps, after a fashion, and managed to take down a man he himself had been after. She'd also prematurely finished her military career at a rank only one below his own, although her regiment in no way compared to the inimitable SAS. The Special Air Service were so tough that they often went overseas to train other nation's Special Forces. The only ones anywhere near as brutally efficient were the Russian Alpha Group and the US Navy Seals. Sarah herself had passed the entry tests for the SAS but was denied on the basis of her gender. Women did not belong in the Special Forces.

But then she had joined MCU, a joint enterprise between the USA and UK that had promised to be the epitome of counter-terrorism and intelligence. It had initially fallen short, but Sarah's actions helped elevate it to its intended position. Over the last few months, she had watched the various news reports discussing the increased funding and prestige of the organisation and she could not help but feel satisfied. She knew the men and women who worked at MCU were hardworking and dedicated, and it pleased her to hear of their increased prosperity.

"We have a new mission," her father said. "Are you in or out?"

Sarah put down her sandwich and cleared her throat. "I finally stop being a hostage and now you want me to take a job with you?"

"I want nothing, Sarah. You are my daughter and duty demands I offer you a chance to do something with your life. With that face you have no chance of finding a man, so at least I can no longer blame you for failing to settle down. If military is your chosen path, I promise you will find no greater vocation than the one I am offering you."

"What's the job?" she asked.

"A manhunt. We are to apprehend a doctor and return him to the South African government who want him for biological attacks on the border towns of their country."

"This doctor has killed people?"

"Many."

Sarah stood up, brushed bread crumbs off her lap. "Okay, I'm in."

The famously morose Major Stone actually managed a slight smile. "Then let's get you into something suitable. We leave on the hour."

Sarah was hustled into an old locker room that had probably once belonged to the staff of whatever business once operated inside the warehouse. She was given a set of combat fatigues to change into and then, once she was dressed, was led back out into the middle of the warehouse's main floor. A trail of blood snaked a path to wherever Rat had scurried off to.

The grey haired, ponytailed man, whose forehead she had sliced, motioned for her to join him at a bench in the centre of the room. He beamed at her, despite the thick bandage taped to his forehead.

“Sorry about that,” she said, pointing to his bandage.

“Hey, I was about to do far worse to you, so forget about it.”

Sarah shrugged. “Fair enough. I’m Sarah.”

“Of course you are. I’m Ollie.”

Sarah frowned.

“What’s wrong?”

“Nothing, you just don’t seem like an Ollie.”

“Call me what you like. I don’t mind.”

“No, Ollie is fine.”

Ollie yanked a tarpaulin off the bench and Sarah whistled at what she saw.

“Top of the line stuff,” he explained, running an appreciative hand over the assortment of firearms and ammunition.

Sarah spotted a familiar 9mm SIG and picked it up. “Mind if I take this one?”

“Sure. The boys are too manly to go for the P226, they prefer something bigger like a .45, but I always stock it because it’s a nice shooter and easy to conceal. I’ve used it a time or two myself, so it’s well looked after.”

Sarah could see the truth of it. The small, black pistol gleamed with a thin layer of oil and the cocking action was the smoothest she’d ever felt. There was even a delicate laser sight attached to the bottom of the muzzle.

Ollie picked up a sheath with the handle of a Ka-Bar knife sticking out the top. “Back-up,” he said, handing it to her. “US Marines swear by ‘em.”

Sarah took the sheath and fastened it to her utility belt. All of a sudden she felt like she was acting in some play. Only hours before she had been a prisoner and now she was suited and booted like a GI Joe. It was all a bit surreal.

Her father came up from the far end of the warehouse, followed by the rest of his men, all suited up in the same combat uniforms as Sarah; even Rat, who now walked as if uninjured. Whatever painkiller they had given him was stronger than anything over the counter. The weasely man glared when he saw her.

Sarah's father took the floor, his men standing to attention. "Alright, men," he barked. "We have a new team member and, while she may be a woman, she is my daughter also, with a set of balls almost as big as my own."

There was sprinkling of laughter from everybody except Rat.

"Now," Major Stone continued. "Sarah took a few lumps out of a couple of you, but remember that you all went through similar trials of initiation once upon a time. All is fair. There will be no grudges." He shot a quick glance to Rat, who recoiled. "Our next target is a doctor by the name of Alistair Krenshaw. He is wanted for using human test subjects on the borders of South Africa. He is a suspected terrorist with designs on biological warfare. It is believed the atrocities he committed in South Africa were trial experiments for something much bigger. He has been back, working in the UK for two years now, an expert in his field. The South African government has not forgotten or forgiven his crimes, though. We have a sighting on him nearby and we are going to pick him up in a nice quick 'stop and grab.' No casualties. No unnecessary attention."

Sarah swallowed. Never having served under her father before, this was the first time she'd witnessed him in action. The complete respect and attention of his men was something she could never hope to emulate. He was one of them, yet above them in every way.

Major Stone marched over to the weapons bench and picked up a Colt Commander with a walnut grip, then cocked it with ease. “We have fought and beaten men of all kinds,” he said. “We have fought entire armies and won. We have killed kings and sultans, men who thought themselves Gods, yet were forced to weep as we brought them crashing down to earth. We are peerless. Superior to marines, paratroopers, and even the SAS itself. We are better than them all. We are without equal and charged with the simple tasks of running down a little doctor in a white coat. The poor bastard is going to piss himself.”

Everybody laughed, except Sarah who was trying to comprehend how this small band of mercenaries could compare themselves to the likes of the SAS.

Major Stone also remained deadly serious and barked an order. “Let’s move out, men.”

Sarah tried to speak with her father, but he turned and marched away before she had chance. Ollie stood beside her instead, smiling kindly. “Don’t worry,” he said. “I got your back.”

Sarah didn’t reply. She followed after the other men, still utterly confused by how she’d suddenly been inducted into her absent father’s private army. Somehow it felt like things were only going to get more confusing.

-9-

Dr Hart was still sobbing in Howard's arms when help finally arrived. It was only a couple of nurses, but Howard was still glad to see them, for they would be far more useful in dealing with the situation than he. Did Dr Hart have AIDS now, or was HIV different? He cursed himself for being so ignorant as not to know. Dr Krenshaw had a point about the West caring little about maladies which did not affect them. The public knew more about the top ten pop chart than it did the top ten deadliest diseases.

"The syringe could have been full of water," he said soothingly to Dr Hart, who continued to cling to him desperately. "It was probably a bluff. A good one because it worked. There didn't even need to be anything dangerous inside the syringe for him to make me back off. I'm sure you're fine. It's okay. It's..." His mouth kept moving but he had idea what words to say.

Dr Hart tried to get a hold of herself, turning her sobs into choking shudders. "G-G-Go...go after him."

Howard took a moment but then understood. He couldn't help Dr Hart, but he could sure as hell go after Dr Krenshaw and bring him to justice. If the syringe had been a bluff, the quickest way to find out would be to put Krenshaw's balls in a vice and ask him. He placed the doctor into the concerned care of the two nurses and clenched his fists. "Dr Krenshaw. Where did he go?"

"Towards the car park out back," one of the nurses replied. "He stopped by the staffroom to grab his briefcase but then went out the fire exit. You may still catch him."

Howard took off like a horse out the gates. He spotted a sign for the staff car park and careened around the corridors towards it. Even before he made it outside he spotted Krenshaw through the wide glass doors. The doctor was running for his life but was skinny and unfit, carrying what looked like a heavy briefcase. He was beating it across the car park, but Howard was right out the door after him. This time, he had no qualms about pulling out his gun and firing it. He aimed a round into the air.

Krenshaw froze in his tracks, crouching down and turning slowly to face Howard. A couple of bystanders leapt for cover behind their cars.

"Give yourself up, Doctor. Or I'll be forced to shoot you."

Krenshaw didn't look afraid. In fact he seemed amused. In his free hand he held a small glass cylinder.

Howard stayed where he was but kept his gun levelled. "What do you have in your hand, Doctor?"

Krenshaw's lips drew back like a curtain into the delighted grimace of a corpse. "Just a concoction I whipped up. Weaponised Dengue Fever, if you must know. Symptoms start with fever, headaches, nausea and vomiting, before progressing to a rash and fluid in the chest. The beauty of this particular strain is that it is highly symptomatic. You see, the more typical strain affects less than one-quarter of infected patients. This will infect over 90% with the most severe case. I carry it with me everywhere. Call it an insurance policy. You try to stop me and I smash the phial, which contains a highly concentrated dose of the disease. It may not cause an epidemic, but it will, at the very least, infect you and me, and perhaps a few dozen sick children inside this hospital."

"Have you not already infected them with something nasty?" asked Howard. He dared not take another step forward and was forced to stall for time. Maybe he could shoot the doctor without the phial smashing, but the fear of what was inside escaping made his blood run too cold to try.

"Alas, no," said Krenshaw. "I was just about to begin my rounds. You see, I like to do my most important work at night and evening is nearly upon us. Morning and afternoon seem like queer times to give people death sentences, don't you agree?"

Howard felt sick. "You were going to infect a bunch of children. You're mad."

"I am very sane, I assure you. In fact it takes a huge level of sanity to make the sacrifices I am making. I want to change the world for the better. Infecting a bunch of sickly white children with HIV is a means to an end. They would get the best care, maybe even live full lives, but the fear would be enough to get this country to pay attention."

"Your mission is over, Doctor. Just hand the phial over and give yourself up."

"Hand it over? Are you so sure you want to take this from me? You have gone quite a striking shade of alabaster."

Howard tried to swallow, but there was a lump in his throat. He spoke in a squawk. "Nobody else is getting sick today, Doctor. This isn't the way."

"It is the only way." Krenshaw tossed the phial into the air.

Howard felt his eyes almost fall out of his head as he watched the small glass bottle arc towards him. His legs tried to carry him away, to run, but he knew it was wrong thing to do, so, with a diving lunge, he threw himself forwards instead. The phial was tiny, but as it tumbled it caught the dimming sunlight and glinted. It gave Howard something to focus on. He hit the pavement hard, chin striking the ground and sending him dizzy. For a few seconds, he forgot himself and lay there in a daze. When he got his wits back he panicked and looked around urgently. He opened up his hands and almost wept when he saw the intact phial clutched in his right fist. His relief turned to fury, though, when he saw the word INSULIN printed on the label. It had been a bluff.

Howard clambered back to his feet, ignoring the spike of pain in his left kneecap where it had struck the pavement. Krenshaw had already made a run for it and had gained a good lead. A parked car up ahead blinked and beeped as the doctor unlocked it with his key fob. There was too much distance between them now for Howard to get to Krenshaw before the doctor hopped in his car and drove away.

Howard brought up his gun, drew a bead, and fired. His round struck the bumper of a car and ricocheted. There were still bystanders hiding in cover and they yelled out in fright now. Howard couldn't risk them getting hit. He lowered his gun and sprinted, hoping against hope that Krenshaw would fail to escape in time. But Krenshaw was almost at his car and seemed to realise he was home-free. He turned around to smirk at Howard.

"Until next time," the doctor gloated, clutching the briefcase to his chest like it was a prize.

There was the sudden screech of skidding tyres.

Two jet-black vans pulled up behind Krenshaw, making the doctor spin around in fright and stumble on his heels. Two burly men in balaclavas hopped out of one of the vans and grabbed Krenshaw before he even knew what was happening, then they bundled him inside the van and held him down on the floor as he struggled. A third person hopped out the front of the other van and ran around to close the side door of the other. This person wasn't wearing a balaclava and was, in fact, a woman.

Howard tripped and stumbled, before stopping completely. In front of him was a woman who'd gone missing more than four months ago and not been heard from since. A former colleague.

Sarah noticed Howard standing there and froze with the same shocked expression that he no doubt wore on his own face. The driver of the van shouted at her and she got moving again, slamming the side door shut of the first van before hopping back into the front passenger seat of the other. Then both vans took off, tyres squealing as they took off around the corner and disappeared.

Howard stood rooted to the spot for so long that he began to shiver from the cold. He couldn't believe who he had just seen: Captain Sarah Stone.

-10-

Howard found Dr Hart sitting inside a small waiting room with a sofa and coffee machine. There was a nurse beside her, rubbing her back as she prodded anxiously at the red spot on her neck. The nurse left when Howard entered.

"Are you okay?" Howard asked Dr Hart. She was a pretty woman, not much over forty, but right now she was haggard and grey and her blonde hair seemed almost white. She didn't say anything in reply to him, just stared at a spot on the wall, barely blinking.

"Krenshaw was bluffing," said Howard enthusiastically. He plucked the insulin phial from his pocket and showed it to her. "He convinced me this was Dengue Fever but it's just plain old Insulin. The syringe he stabbed you with was probably nothing."

"They've pried open his locker," she eventually said, a detached numbness to her voice. "You should go take a look."

Howard took her advice and left her alone. On his way to find a nurse to direct him, he took out his mobsat and placed a call though to the Earthworm, MCU's base of operations. He went straight through to Director Palu.

"Howard. Update me."

Howard cleared his throat and began. "My investigation at Whiteknight seemed to confirm the epidemic was engineered and led me to a suspect named Dr Alistair Krenshaw. I tracked him down to Reading Children's Hospital where he was planning to carry out a second act of terror. This time a mass infection of the HIV virus on already sick children."

"You stopped it?"

"I did, but Krenshaw managed to escape. He was...abducted."

There was a brief pause before Palu spoke. "Abducted?"

"Two black vans pulled up right behind Krenshaw and two men leapt out and dragged him into the back. Palu... Sarah was with them. Sarah Stone."

The next pause was even longer.

"I know," said Howard. "It doesn't make any sense, but it was her, I swear. There's no doubt in my mind."

"Then, where the hell has she been? And who is she working with?"

Howard stopped in the middle of the corridor and leaned up against the wall, groaning. "I have no idea, but whoever she is with has the doctor and I am positive Krenshaw is our man. What is Sarah involved in?"

"Do you have a description of the men she was with?"

"No. They were wearing balaclavas."

"I'll have Jessica check CCTV for the area. I'm sure the hospital will have something."

"Check the rear car park," said Howard. "That's where the black vans arrived."

"Do you have any other leads?"

Howard sighed. "Not yet. I'm about to search Krenshaw's locker and see what I find. Can you have someone gather everything we have on the doctor?"

"Of course. Good work, Howard. We'll catch Krenshaw; only a matter of time."

"I'll keep you updated." Howard ended the call, found a nurse, and asked to be taken to Krenshaw's locker. Inside the staff changing area, there was another nurse already there waiting for him.

"This is the doctor's locker," the woman told him, indicating which one she meant.

The locker was hanging slightly ajar, so Howard fondled the edge and swung it open wider. Inside was not a comforting sight. The top metal shelf was stacked with phials of clear liquid. A bundle of unsealed syringes right beside them.

"Do we know what's inside them?" asked Howard of the nurse.

"We'll need to get them to a lab, but I can tell you they aren't legally endorsed."

"What do you mean?"

"I mean that these didn't come from an approved pharmaceutical supplier. They're either black market or, worse, homemade. There're no labels, no serial numbers. Even the bottles aren't NHS issue. Whatever is in these phials didn't come through the system."

Howard thanked the nurse and asked her to bring Dr Hart to him. She would still be understandably distraught, but he needed answers.

She appeared five minutes later, back in charge of her emotions, yet slightly timid in voice. "What can I do for you, Agent Hopkins?"

"Is there any way of finding out what is inside these phials?"

"They can be tested for HIV fairly quickly, if that's what you mean? I'll contact the lab and fast track it myself."

Howard nodded grimly. "What are you going to do about yourself?"

She shrugged, almost as if she didn't care. Howard thought it more likely the numbness of shock, or maybe she just knew there was little she could do. "I'll have to start on anti-retroviral immediately," she explained, "whether I am infected or not. It will take three months or so before any blood tests will be reliable."

Howard put himself in the doctor's shoes and felt quite sick. It was going to be a long three months of hell while she was forced to wait for results on whether or not she was gravely ill. "Krenshaw admitted he never managed to infect any of the children," he said, hoping it would give her some solace.

"You let him get away, though?"

Howard didn't take it personally. If anyone had the right to apportion blame, it was Dr Hart. "I'm sorry. I have all my people working on it. We'll get him, I promise." He chose not to complicate matters by explaining about the black vans and his former colleague appearing to snatch Krenshaw away just as he was about to get away.

"I need to go back to Whiteknight," she said, looking away from him. "I can get treatment there and I need to get back to trying to deal with the Ebola epidemic."

Howard nodded. Any friendliness that had existed between them was now gone, extinguished the moment Krenshaw plunged a syringe into her neck. Howard had failed the woman, and could tell that Dr Hart regretted ever having met him. He regretted it, too, but for different reasons.

"If you need anything..."

Dr Hart nodded, turned around, and left.

For a while, Howard stood alone in the locker room, staring at the collection of unlabelled liquids in the locker and shuddering. Eventually a nurse came in and started loading everything into a padded yellow crate. "I'll get this sent straight to the pathology lab in Slough," she told him. "If you leave me your details, I'll have them call you with the results."

"Thank you." Howard left her his details and thanked her, then exited the hospital as quickly as he could and stood out in the fresh air of the newly arrived night. It felt good to be in the open, out of the claustrophobic confines of the hospital. His breaths were longer, steadier, and, as he walked over to the curb where his MCU Range Rover was parked, he began to feel better. He wondered where Dr Hart had gone and how she was getting back to Whiteknight. Running, probably, if it got her away from him. The thought of her alone and scared brought tears to Howard's eyes as he finally allowed himself to acknowledge how much today's ordeal had upset him. He'd been relentlessly afraid the entire time, but it was Dr Hart who had been hurt.

A shrill ring caused Howard to flinch from his thoughts and pull his mobsat from his coat. He answered the call and placed it to his ear. "Hopkins."

"Howard!" It was Jessica Bennett, a Georgia gal transferred from MCU America and currently his closest colleague, as well as probably the smartest person he knew. She, too, was a doctor but specialised in the mind rather than the body. "I checked the hospital CCTV and got a good look at the black vans. I saw the men you saw. Was that really Sarah?"

"I'm certain of it. I looked her right in the eye. Not like she could be mistaken for anyone else with those scars of hers."

"I thought she was dead."

"Me too. Looks like everything we assumed was wrong. She's working with someone and they have Krenshaw."

"It's her daddy," Jessica blurted out, her southern state accent more prevalent when she wasn't speaking slowly.

Howard unlocked the Range Rover and got in behind the wheel where it was warmer and quieter. He adjusted the mobsat against his ear and then continued the conversation. "Her father? How do you know?"

Jessica told him. "The men in the back of the vans were wearing balaclavas, but I got a clear view at the driver who wasn't wearing a mask of any kind. I ran his face through the Interpol and military databases and it came up as a wanted war criminal, Major Jonathan Stone."

Howard flopped back against the leather driver's seat. "That makes no sense. Sarah's father is a Major in the Army. Isn't he SAS?"

"He was," said Jessica, "but he went AWOL with a group of his men almost a year ago. He was last seen in Syria, taking out an ISIS leader."

"Well, that's good. He's still on our side by the sound of it."

"No. He killed the ISIS leader on behalf of a Saudi Prince who lost a cousin in a rebel attack. He was paid to do it."

"He's a mercenary."

"Looks like it. He's been off the radar since he assassinated that ISIS leader, and Interpol had assumed he'd gone into hiding."

Howard rubbed at his eyes, feeling exhauster. "What has Sarah got herself into?"

"I don't know, but if her daddy has Krenshaw, it's because somebody else is paying for him."

"Any background on Krenshaw yet?"

"Not much. I've requested his work records from World Health Alliance who employed him during his time in Africa. They haven't gotten back to me yet. He's been back in the country for two years and has held senior posts in the NHS the entire time. There's nothing to suggest he's dangerous."

Howard huffed. "Believe me, he's dangerous. I stood there and watched him inject an innocent woman with HIV."

"My Lord."

"Yeah," said Howard. "We need to get this guy, Jessica."

"I have Mandy and Mattock checking out Krenshaw's home and his office at Whiteknight, to see if we can find any clue as to what his next move might have been. I'll keep working on Sarah's daddy, see if I can figure out where he might be operating out of. I ran the plates on one of the black vans, but it came back as a stolen Nissan. They'll probably shed the plates as soon as they get chance."

Howard cursed. "I swear, if I get a hold of Sarah..."

"Don't assume she's on the wrong side of this. We don't have the facts yet."

Howard sighed. "No, you're right. At least Krenshaw is out of action for now. I would hate to think he was still at large with a dirty syringe full of whatever he planned on unleashing next. Whiteknight hospital is a nightmare, Jessica. Two hundred people dying in agony, dozens already dead. Krenshaw planned on infecting a children's hospital with HIV. The man is capable of anything when it comes to his mission. He wants the UK to see the suffering of Africa first-hand. He thinks his work will result in money and effort being diverted to finding a cure for all of these diseases."

Jessica moaned. "He's a martyr. There's no worse kind of madman."

"I know. He doesn't want anything but to carry out his mission. If he manages to get free, there's no limit to what he might do."

"Then let's just hope that whatever Sarah is doing works out for the best."

Howard thought about Sarah for a moment. He had worked with her for less than a month, but he knew that as much as she was aggressive and unhelpful, she was a good person deep at heart. She had a strong instinct to protect the innocent, but she also hated the United Kingdom for what it did to her. If she was with her father there was no way of knowing what she was involved in or what she was thinking. If they were both carrying a grudge towards their country, there was no telling what they might do.

Howard had an idea. “Jessica, don’t focus your efforts on Sarah’s father, focus it on Sarah herself. If we can work out what happened to her — how she disappeared — we might be able to figure out how and why she ended up with her father.”

“But we already searched high and low for her,” said Jessica. “We couldn’t find anything. You, yourself, followed every lead you could find.”

“We assumed then that a remnant of Hesbani’s crew was involved with her disappearance. Now we know different. Look at known associates of Major Stone, particularly the men who deserted with him. If we can find anything on them we might be able to link it to Sarah and find out where she is.”

“Okay, Howard. I’m on it. You stay safe, okay?”

“I’ll do my best. Just get back to me as soon as you have something. I want to put a stop to this before Sarah ends up doing something she’ll regret.”

“Sarah never struck me as a woman who regretted anything.”

“Then you don’t know Sarah at all. The woman I knew was nothing but a list of regrets. Let’s not give her any chance to add to it.”

-11-

That had been Howard, she was sure of it. He'd been standing there only twenty-metres away from Sarah, watching while she helped kidnap a man. A man he, too, had been after. What did the MCU want with Krenshaw? Was she impeding a government operation by intervening and getting to the doctor first? Did she even care?

Sarah sat up front with her father in the first of the two black vans, staring at the back streets as they slunk away from the main roads.

"Did you get a look at that man in the car park," her father asked. "He saw your face. You should never got out of the van without a mask. What the Hell were you doing?"

"I didn't think. I was just trying to help. Your men were making a scene, and excuse me if my wits aren't that sharp. I've been locked up with nothing to do for four months."

"There are no excuses for mistakes. You've compromised this entire unit. That man looked like a police officer."

"He's MCU," Sarah said. "I know him. He knows me."

Her father punched the top of the steering wheel. "Damn it,

Sarah. My unit can only exist if it fades in and out of the shadows. If you've been recognised then your MCU boyfriend has something to work with. It's not like it would be hard to get a positive ID on a face like yours, even if he hadn't known you already."

Sarah looked away, out of her window, anything to avoid the burning glare of her father. "He isn't my boyfriend. I worked with him for a couple of weeks at most."

Her father glanced at her for a moment, then stopped the van at the edge of a side street. Before he spoke he let out a disappointed grunt. "If you've been ID'd then we need to get this mission done quickly and disappear. There's no going back for you now, Sarah. You can't change your mind because you know too much now about me and my men. If I let you leave, they can use you to get to me."

Sarah frowned. "Who exactly would be trying to get to you? What have you done?"

"My duty," he said. "A grievous crime in this day and age. I'm serious, Sarah. You're in this now. This is your life. The choice has been taken away from you. Do you understand? You can't go back to your old life."

Sarah grunted. "I don't have an old life to go back to. This isn't about my choice being made for me, though, is it? It's about your choice being made. You're stuck with me now. You can't get rid of me, even if you want to."

Major Stone glared at her so hard that she shrank in her seat. "Sarah, there's always a way to get rid of someone, even a daughter. Don't forget that."

Sarah opened her mouth to speak but dared not. She felt like she was sitting beside a great venomous lizard ready to strike at the slightest movement. Was there any love her father held for her at all?

He pulled away from the curb and headed back out onto the main road. Twenty-minutes later, they were back at the warehouse's courtyard, where they parked up next to the bright red e-type Jaguar. The courtyard was enclosed and hidden from the roadside, which made the warehouse an excellent hideout – for that, Sarah realised, was what it was. Everybody got out of the vans and Dr Krenshaw, clutching a briefcase tightly to his chest, was bundled into the warehouse. There he was taken away by her father and a pair of men she had yet to speak to.

"He's getting your old room," said Ollie.

"Then I hope he doesn't fancy watching the telly."

Ollie didn't understand her comment – how could he? – so he just smiled and headed off.

Rat came up to her a minute later, the expression on his face far less kind. "I hear you're with us for the duration. Good. Gives me time to get a little payback."

Sarah rolled her eyes like he was nothing but a mere irritation. "You should be thanking me. I was going to kill you."

"I'm not as easy to kill as you think, sweetheart."

"All men die the same when you cut their throats. Maybe next time I won't aim for your shoulder."

Rat sneered and walked away.

Sarah milled around the warehouse, glad to be alone for a while. From all of the oily workbenches, she assumed the warehouse had once been concerned with some kind of assembly. The odd scrap of metal here and there further suggested that this place once housed bored employees fitting things together. Now it was a staging area for a team of ex-SAS. How things changed. Six months ago, she had almost had her life on track. Now she felt utterly directionless. Her father's orders were the only thing steering her, and that was not necessarily something she was comfortable with. She held no great love for her father, had not known him well enough to have such depth of emotion, yet there was a yearning inside of her, a deep desire to gain the respect — if not love — of Major Stone. It was fantasy, most likely, but the little girl inside of her couldn't let it go. After all that had happened, a hug from her daddy could mend so much, yet the thought of it happening felt childishly naive. Her father was a brutal killer, not a hugger.

It was a while before the others began filtering back to the main floor of the warehouse. Sarah took the opportunity to make the acquaintance of the rest of the group. The black man she'd beaten up upon her escape was named Rupert, of all things. He was embarrassed about the incident more than angry and admitted that her ruse of insanity had utterly bewildered him. For a hired killer, he was friendly, but there was an air of regimentally to him that suggested he was an institutionalised military man. Men like Rupert could not go back to ordinary life. There were two other men. Graves, a man who was older than her father by at least a decade, but his wiry frame and leather skin only added to his aura of lethality – like a wizened cobra. Spots was a much younger man, with the worst acne Sarah had ever seen. He smiled more than Graves did but not by much. Both men oozed with the coiled menace of warriors-on-standby, ready to strike out and kill at a moment's notice, just waiting for their next order. They were brutal soldiers; elite grunts.

Sarah made her way over to Ollie, who she deemed the least likely to suddenly attack her. The man seemed out of place amongst the others, less a soldier and less a killer. He smiled at her warmly when she approached him. "Hey, Sarah. You doing okay?"

"Just a bit Alice in Wonderland, you know?"

"Curiouser and curiouser," he replied.

"Exactly. So what are we going to do with the doctor now that we have him?"

"Ask your father. He tells us what to do when he needs us to do it. We don't ask questions."

Sarah frowned. "You don't ask questions? Why would you not want to know what you're fighting for?"

"I know what I'm fighting for," he said. "Your father. I'm not ex-SAS like the other guys, never even served, but I'm just as willing to jump into the flames for what I believe in."

"If you never served, then how do you know my father?"

Ollie smiled at her as if he admired her questioning nature. "I'm an old friend of his, but I was never in the forces. I was a teacher."

Sarah almost barked at him, so unexpected were his words. "You were a teacher?"

Ollie chuckled. "Yes, I was a teacher. I went to teach in Sri Lanka in my early twenties, married a local woman, Darla. She was a teacher, too. There was a long civil war going on in Sri Lanka, back then. The insurgents were the Tamil Tigers. One day they decided to take our school hostage in order to make demands of the Government. The government refused to even negotiate and a firefight ensued. The Tamil Tigers, used the children as human shields and barricaded the windows. We were trapped there as hostages for three days. Even when they cut of the water and electricity, turning the building into a sweating furnace, the Tigers did not submit. They were prepared to die before giving themselves up. Eventually the school burned. My wife didn't make it out of her classroom. I was trapped in another part of the building but managed to get out. When I finally got to her, she was already dead."

Sarah felt her left eye twitched, setting off a flare of pain in her scared eyelid. "I'm sorry," she said quietly. "Seems like everywhere you turn these days there are terrorists wrecking lives."

"It wasn't the Tamil Tigers who killed my wife," Ollie told her.

"It was the government retaliation. They firebombed the entire school and let it burn. They wanted to kill the rebels more than they valued the life of their children. About half of us made it out alive, but the rest were left to burn. Nowadays, the Sri Lankan government boasts about how they are the only modern nation to entirely oust its terrorists. But the truth is, the terrorists are the ones in charge."

"I'm sorry," said Sarah.

"Anyway," Ollie continued cheerily, despite the sadness in my eyes. "I moved back home and resumed contact with your father. He gave me purpose; a chance to eliminate the types of men who killed my lovely Darla. I'm not a born killer, Sarah, but I've turned my hand to it pretty well. In fact, I quite enjoy it. I don't know what that means for my soul."

Sarah understood the quenching pleasure of revenge and patted him on the shoulder. "Our soul isn't in jeopardy when we kill bad people. It's in jeopardy when we stop protecting the good ones."

"Alright, men," Major Stone barked, marching onto the warehouse floor. "Gather up."

Everyone stopped talking and assembled.

"Well done on another successful mission," he said. "We have the doctor safe and secure and I've just gotten the clearances we need to get him — and us — out of the country."

"We're leaving?" said Rat unhappily, now favouring his shoulder again and letting the pain show in his voice. "We only just came back home."

Major Stone shot him a stony glance. "Your home is this unit, Rat. You gave up any entitlement to a home when you defected, as did I. Unfortunately, my daughter has been ID'd, which means we need to disappear for a while. Once we complete our mission and get out of the country, the heat will die off and we will come back."

Sarah looked down at the floor as angry glances shot her way.

"So, where are we going, Major?" asked Ollie in a tone that suggested he had little problem with having to leave.

"We're heading to Libya. We'll land in Tripoli and head along the coast to Tunisia where we can pose as tourists and soak up the sun for a while."

There was a quick cheer and suddenly Sarah didn't feel so bad anymore. In fact, a bit of sunbathing sounded pretty good to her, although she wasn't so sure her face and gender would make life easy in the more rural parts of the country. There was one other thing on her mind. "I thought Dr Krenshaw was wanted by the South African government. So why are we heading to Tripoli?"

Her father turned his glare to her and once again made her feel tiny. "Which is why they are having their people collect the doctor in Libya. South Africa doesn't want to advertise their involvement in an unsanctioned manhunt. It's a lot easier to conduct ourselves quietly in a place like Libya."

Sarah was quiet.

Her father straightened up and lifted his chin. "Right, clear off, you lot. Our flights are at 0600 from Heathrow, so get your socks on by 0400."

Everyone dispersed.

Her father marched away and Sarah went after him, asking, "What do we do once we get to Libya?"

Major Stone turned on her and bore into her with his emerald eyes. "I need for you to understand something for me, Sarah. You do not ask questions. I give orders and you follow them. You are a soldier now, not my daughter, so when I dismiss you, do not chase after me and start demanding to know things I have elected not to tell you."

Sarah growled. "Are you capable of being anything other than an arsehole?"

"I'll let you have that one, because you're new. You don't want to see what happens next time. Now get out of my sight."

Sarah clenched her fists as her father — her superior — marched away into one of the offices. When she finally calmed down enough to walk away, Rat was laughing at her. He was too far away to have made out the words, but he could obviously tell she had just received a dressing down.

"You won't get any special treatment around here," he said.

"I don't need any," she said.

"I would've been the first to help you settle in if you'd been a little nicer to me. Then you went and stabbed me, you bitch."

Sarah marched up to Rat and stood right in his face. He wasn't afraid of her. In fact, he was snickering with delight.

"Say that word again," she said.

"You think you're something really hot, don't you? Don't forget I watched you rot in a cell for four months. I know you're nothing but a weak, ordinary woman. You won't last with us. We're men."

Sarah grinned, repressing a sudden urge to bite the man's face and listen to him squeal. "And don't forget I saw how weak and stupid you are. You were the guard who let me escape. I played you like a fucking flute."

"Shut up, you ugly bitch."

Sarah smashed her elbow into Rat's collarbone, right where she had stabbed him earlier. He hit the floor, bellowing as she kicked him in the stomach.

"I did warn you," she said, looking down at him. "I always warn you."

Ollie came up beside and moved her away. "You're not making any friends," he said to her privately. "Rat doesn't look like much, but he holds grudges and follows them through. Be careful."

Sarah shrugged. "What's the worst he can do?"

Ollie wasn't joking when he spoke. "He can put a bullet in your back the next time he's supposed to be watching it, and I would hate to see that."

Sarah looked over at Rat, who had gotten back to his feet and was glaring at her. If he wasn't an enemy before, he was now.

"Why do you even care?"

Ollie became flustered before he managed to answer. "Guess it's just nice having someone new around. Gets a bit tiring being surrounded by vicious killers night and day."

"I'm a vicious killer," she said.

Ollie nodded. "Less vicious, and that makes you a saint around here."

Sarah chuckled. "What have I got myself into?"

"A dysfunctional family."

"Yeah," she said. "The Manson family."

-12-

The Earthworm was abuzz despite the late hour. Since the MCU had its funding renewed, a major recruitment operation had been put into place. The tail section of the facility was now fully manned by twenty-eight data analysts who used the very latest in technology. Their surveillance capabilities were on par with America's NSA and the hardware it ran on was newer than anything NASA owned. In less than a year it would be obsolete, such was the nature of surveillance technology.

The Earthworm's middle section housed the infirmary, the dorms, and a host of offices and training rooms. Any member of MCU could access this area, but Howard kept on going until he was at the head section, where only Level 1 operatives could enter. He pressed his thumb against the scanner and went inside. It was like entering the belly of a great beast. Soft lighting merged with the blinking switches of whirring computers and all four walls were lined with monitors displaying graphs, charts, and various other readouts. In the centre of the electric grotto was the MCU's senior team: Director Palu, Strike Team Leader Mattock, and Dr Jessica Bennett. Howard, too, was part of that leadership team.

Jessica got up and hugged him, not unusual since they'd worked closely together over the last few months. "I'm glad you're okay," she told him. "You sounded bad on the phone."

Howard gave her an affectionate pat on the arm. "It's not pretty at Whiteknight. I prefer traditional terrorists who just blow things up. At least that's quick and final. The people I saw at Whiteknight are suffering, not knowing if they're going to live or die. Krenshaw was going to give an even more protracted death sentence to a bunch of children. He was going to infect them all with HIV."

"Have we confirmed that yet?" Palu asked him, looking grim yet indefatigable as ever.

Howard nodded. "I got the call from the lab ten minutes ago. The tests were positive, which means Dr Hart, who was trying to help me, might be infected."

Jessica obviously saw how devastating that fact was to him, because she ushered him down onto a chair as though he were an invalid. "HIV is very treatable these days," she told him, "and there's no guarantee Dr Hart will be infected anyway. Early treatment might prevent the virus taking hold."

Howard nodded. "I hope so. Let's just catch Krenshaw, then I'll feel better."

"That's the plan," said Palu. "And we have leads to that effect."

"Is it true you saw Sarah?" Mattock asked Howard.

"Yes."

"Blimey. I was sure the lass was dead. Glad she's not."

Howard was glad to see Sarah alive, too, but not under such circumstances. "We don't know what she's involved in. She helped kidnap Krenshaw."

"If she's really with her father," said Palu. "Then it can't be anything good. We've received some unofficial reports from local Intel that Major Stone hasn't just gone rogue, but has allied himself with our enemies. Our Iranian ambassador was assassinated eight months ago at a time when Sarah's father was rumoured to be in the country. A local resistance group swears Stone did it. The resulting turmoil led to the embassy being abandoned and our people ousted, something the Iranian government no doubt enjoyed immensely."

"I know Major Stone," said Mattock. "Served under him in Afghanistan and Iraq. He's an unlovable sod with barely a care for anyone, but he lives by his honour. If he's gone rogue, then it's for a reason he deems valid. If he's helping foreign governments, it's because he thinks it's for the greater good. His men will be following him because they believe in whatever cause he has sold them."

"Sarah, too?" said Jessica.

Mattock nodded. "It's her father. As much as he's a cold-hearted sonofabitch, it's obvious the poor girl loves him."

Jessica frowned. "Don't think 'poor girl' is an appropriate way to describe Sarah Stone. She has bigger chestnuts than you do."

Mattock grinned. "Bloody right she does, but she's a good egg deep down, I know it. Whatever monkey business her father's into, she's probably just been dragged along for the ride. Especially after what one of the analysts showed me."

"What?" Howard quickly asked.

Mattock nodded at Jessica. "Show him."

Jessica tapped a command into the laptop in front of her and one of the wall-mounted monitors started playing a video.

"We did what you told us to do," Mattock explained. "We ran checks on all of Major Stone's men who went AWOL with him. We got a hit on an active mobile phone at the time Sarah went missing. It was unregistered, but we ran voice analysis against all of Major Stone's men and managed to match a phone call from

Corporal Patrick Rattiger. His military record reads more like a rap sheet. At the time of his desertion he was up for court martial, accused of slaughtering unarmed prisoners taken from the ranks of a Taliban outshoot. He cut off both their hands and left them to bleed to death from the stumps. The mobile phone we traced is dead now so we can't track it, but on the day Sarah went missing, Rattiger made a call outside Forest Glade Cemetery."

Howard recognised the name immediately. "That's where Bradley was buried."

Bradley was a former colleague who had died during a previous mission when the Earthworm was attacked. He had been intending to quit but never got the chance.

Mattock pointed. "This is a CCTV feed from an office building across the road. Look at the top left of the picture."

Howard leaned forward. "That's Sarah! She was at Bradley's funeral?"

"Looks like it," said Jessica. "I don't know why she didn't come join the rest of us."

"Maybe she was planning to," said Mattock. "But watch what happens."

Howard was agog as he watched Sarah's father appear, flanked by two brutish men. Sarah didn't see them until it was too late. She was struck on the head and bundled into the back of a familiar-looking black van, gone before she even knew what was happening."

"Her father abducted her? But why?"

"We don't know," said Palu. "Nobody currently knows what is going on with Major Stone. He is a completely unknown entity since he went rogue. Sarah, however, is still one of us, until we know otherwise. I don't care how brief her time on this team was, she helped us, and without her efforts the MCU would be no more. We owe her."

Jessica sat back in her chair and folded her arms. "I agree. I did everything I could to find her, but this is the first chance we've gotten to find out what really happened to her."

"I'd like to bring the lass back into the fold," said Mattock. "She'd be much better off with us than her old shite of a dad."

"Then what's our next move?" asked Howard.

It was at this point that Palu smiled. From his laptop he brought up some info on one of the monitors. "The phone that led us to the cemetery stayed in use for another three days. Listed here are the location that calls were made from. Many are from within Greater London."

Howard scanned the list and looked for something to jump out at him. "Are any of these rural areas, or maybe even industrial parks?"

Palu went back to his laptop and spent a few minutes without saying anything. Eventually, he spoke. "There are none rural, but there were six calls made from an area named Leeson on the outskirts of Watford. It's listed as having several warehouses and factories in the vicinity."

"Any of them abandoned?"

Palu tapped in some more commands then looked up with an eyebrow raised. "Yes. M.Hickman Springs has been listed as untenanted for over eighteen-months."

Mattock looked at Howard. "You thinking it's some sort of hideout?"

"If Major Stone is a wanted man he needs somewhere to lay low. This warehouse might be where he's going to ground between missions."

Mattock put his hands on the desk, went to stand up. "I'll get a team together."

Howard waved him back down. "No. I don't think we should go in hard. I don't want to risk Sarah being a casualty. I'll go in alone."

"No, you bloody won't," said Jessica, more partial nowadays to British slang than her own American. "You don't know how many men Major Stone has with him. It's a foolish idea."

"If Sarah is there, I can get to her in private and try to find out what's going on. If Krenshaw is there, going in quiet is far better than provoking a firefight. If he unleashes another of his diseases then at least only I run the risk of being exposed."

"You're assuming Krenshaw is free to act. He is a captive of Major Stone."

Howard grunted. "I'm not assuming anything after what I've been through today."

Mattock still looked ready to get up and leave, but he waited for Palu to speak. "Your call, guvnor."

Palu let out a deep sigh and knitted his fingers together. "This has been a very long day for you, Howard. Are you sure you wouldn't like to sit this one out?"

"I'm fine. I'll rest after I speak with Sarah." He took a deep breath and let it out in a long, drawn out sigh. "Look, I brought Sarah into the MCU, and if she's in trouble then it's my fault. I need to get to her."

Director Palu shook his head. "You're not going alone. Take Jessica with you as back up and stay in radio contact with Mattock's team who will remain close by. The moment things even look like they're turning sour, Mattock moves in."

"Jessica doesn't have the experience for this," said Howard.

Jessica didn't react because she probably agreed with him. She'd only been on a handful of missions, and none had gone flawlessly, although she had handled herself well in all.

"I know Jessica is a little green," agreed Palu, "but if you're having to watch out for her, you're less likely to take risks. That's why she's going with you."

Jessica spoke up now. “I want to see Sarah safe and sound as much as you, Howard. You need backup.”

“Okay, fine, but I’m leaving now, so get ready.”

“I’d suggest wearing a vest,” said Mattock. “Major Stone’s men are trained warriors and I wouldn’t be the least bit surprised if they’re well-armed.”

“Yes,” said Palu. “I expect you all back here alive, so prepare for the worst.”

Howard got up and went over to the door. “One thing you can never prepare for is the worst.”

“Then prepare for lots of highly trained psychopaths trying to kill you,” said Mattock.

Howard smirked. “Now that I can prepare for.”

He left, taking Jessica with him.

-13-

Sarah lay on a cot bed in an oily room full of sharp edges. Perversely, she missed the comfort of the mock bedroom her father had held her in for the four months prior. Originally, the cot bed had been side-by-side with several others in another room, but Ollie had dragged it into a separate room for her to get some privacy away from the men. She didn't know if it was a condescending gesture or one of kindness, but she couldn't deny that she would not have enjoyed sleeping next to the likes of Rat. Not that she could sleep particularly well on her own either. In the windowless darkness, she couldn't even make out her own arm in front of her. It was cold and her skin was grimy, both things non-conducive to sleep, yet she had managed a few hours during the early hours of morning and was fading off again.

Before she had chance to sleep more, she was eventually snapped awake from the gruff holler of her father's voice. She sat up on the bed, disorientated and groggy. The back of her throat and nose seemed fused together and her eyes wept with tiredness, but she was a solider, and as any soldier was trained to do, she shook the cobwebs free and got her head in the game. She pulled on her boots and slipped out into the warehouse's main floor, where she realised that she was the last to arrive. The other men noticed her tardiness but said nothing. Her father, however, glared. The group were all dressed in their civvies, ready to blend in with the crowds.

Dr Krenshaw had been brought before them and looked remarkably well for a prisoner. Despite his ordeal, he was smartly dressed and still had his briefcase. The man's colourless eyes were unmoving above the bony crags of his cheeks and for a moment he took on that familiar corpse-like appearance. This was the man MCU wanted, which meant he was dangerous. She had helped a fugitive escape custody and was now about to smuggle him out of the country.

Rupert nodded to Sarah and handed her a bottle of water, which she swigged from gladly. Spots and Graves blanked her, standing to attention already as they eagerly awaited instruction. Rat, as always, shot daggers at her. His shoulder was patched up beneath his shirt, causing a bulge, but he no longer favoured it. The glazed look to his eye was probably due to whatever strong painkiller he had also taken yesterday.

"We won't be coming back here," said Major Stone. "So if you want it, bring it. Ollie has our exit packages. Get your papers and be ready to leave in ten."

Sarah hung back while the men gathered around Ollie. The last time she had served alongside men like these, she had been their captain. Now she attempted to remain unnoticed, feeling completely out of her depth. When the group dispersed, Ollie nodded at her to come over. He held out a bundle of papers, which she took, surprised to see that it was a passport with her face and first name but a different last name — Reid.

"It's fool proof," Ollie told her.

"How did you get these so quickly?"

"One of your father's contacts in the city. I went out and got them while the rest of you slept."

"You must be knackered?"

Ollie smiled. It wasn't just his hair that was grey but his entire face, yet he seemed to beam bright whenever he smiled, and he had the same glinting emerald eyes of her father. "I haven't had a good night's sleep in ten years."

Sarah ran a finger over her scars. "Yeah, I get that."

Banded together with the passport was a one-way ticket to Libya and a credit card in the name of Sarah Reid. Whoever her father's contact was possessed impressive speed and skill.

Dr Krenshaw headed after her father as he marched towards the warehouse's exit and Sarah frowned, thinking the so-called prisoner should be tied up or under guard. Her father was walking with Krenshaw casually like an old friend. They even seemed to be chatting.

"What did Krenshaw do?" Sarah asked Ollie.

"Made a bunch of people sick. Did you catch the news about the Ebola outbreak in Reading? That was him. I hear your mates at the MCU are after him."

Sarah nodded. "I ran into one of them. Krenshaw must be pretty bad if MCU are hunting him down."

"He's just about the worst," said Ollie. "The type of coward who relies on viruses and diseases to do his dirty work deserves to be put down."

"So what the hell are we doing with him? Why are we getting in the way of his capture and punishment?"

Ollie laughed and patted her on the shoulder, leaving his hand there and saying, "For the money."

Sarah screwed her face up. "There has to be more to this than money."

"Not really. Money allows us to be choosier with our next mission. We can't always fight the good fight, Sarah."

"There is no good fight if we help men like Krenshaw evade capture."

"Life isn't black and white. I wish it was because then I would know if I was one of the good guys or one of the bad. Tell you the truth, I think I might be a little bit of both, but my intentions lean in the right direction. I'm sure you understand that."

Sarah hated to admit it but she did. "I guess we should just try to be more good than bad."

Ollie headed off in the direction her father had gone. Sarah realised she was the only one left in the warehouse now and considered the prospect of staying behind. Sure, Howard had seen her and she had impeded his operation, but she knew the man. Howard would listen if she went to him, but doing so would betray her father. If she did that, she wasn't so sure she would get to carry on living. She was under no illusion that her father lacked the ability to show affection, but she had begun to feel that he could at least grow to respect her. Betraying him now would undo all she had accomplished in the last twenty-four hours.

She just couldn't do it. Her father had served his country a lifetime longer than she had and it would be wrong to second-guess his motives. He said he was doing what was right, and she had no reason to doubt him. Killing bad guys had been her father's entire life, placed ever above his own personal desires. Major Stone deserved trust, not just from her but from anybody who ever served under him.

Sarah swallowed her doubts and hurried out of the warehouse, where everyone else was gathered in the floodlit courtyard. The sky overhead was black and the wind whistled through the battered drainpipes of the building. Krenshaw climbed inside the back of one of the jet black vans of his own volition, a leather briefcase clutched tightly against his chest. Rat and Graves hopped in beside him. Ollie took the driver's seat of the second van while Spots and Rupert jumped in the back and pulled closed the sliding door.

Sarah's father came up beside her and motioned to the long-snouted e-type Jaguar. "You're riding with me," he said.

"Wow, okay." As a child, Sarah had not even been allowed to look at her father's prized classic, so to be getting inside of it was an honour, yet she couldn't help but bring something up. "A little conspicuous, don't you think? Aren't we about to flee the country?"

"Plates are false and the car is registered to a ghost. It's more conspicuous to be driving around in a pair of black vans that have already been spotted by the MCU, which is why the men can go ahead and we'll follow behind."

"I'm honoured to be in the non-expendable car," she said.

Her father grunted. "Don't be. I know that if my men get captured they won't speak. I want you with me."

Sarah rolled her eyes. "God, you can't consider me as anything but a liability, can you? Is it just because I'm a woman, or is there more to it?"

"It's just because you're a woman."

Sarah's mouth dropped open, but anything she was about to say was cut off by the roar of the Jaguar's engine. The two black vans headed out of the courtyard and her father began to follow. They were just about to head out onto the main road, when they were forced to slam on the brakes.

Three black Range Rovers skidded in front of the courtyard's exit, blocking any escape.

Major Stone gripped the steering wheel tightly. "Damn it! It's your friends from the MCU. Did you contact them?"

Sarah growled. "No, I didn't."

Sergeant Mattock and a group of men she didn't recognise leapt out of the Range Rovers and immediately aimed their assault rifles. The sides of the two black vans opened up and Sarah's father's men leapt out and opened fire. Krenshaw scurried into cover near the warehouse but couldn't get inside since the door had locked behind them. Under the harsh glare of the floodlights, he looked once again like a grimacing corpse.

Sarah ducked down beneath the dashboard. Her father opened his door and slid out into cover behind it, pulling out his Colt Commander and letting off a series of eardrum-busting shots.

"I'm not armed," Sarah said, flinching as more gunfire rattled the very air around her.

"Why the hell not?" her father demanded.

"We're heading to the airport," she said. "I didn't think guns were appropriate."

"In the glove compartment."

Sarah flinched as the windscreen shattered and rained glass on her. "What?"

Her father bellowed at her. "In the goddamn glove compartment."

Sarah fiddled with the catch and yanked the glove compartment open. Inside was a Mac-10 and two magazines. An unwieldy and unsophisticated weapon, but perhaps the ideal thing to keep hidden inside a glove compartment. She punched one of the magazines into the handle of the snub nosed machine pistol and crawled out into cover. Bullets pinged the classic Jaguar and she could almost hear her father wince every time it was hit. The MCU were raining down Hell on them. Major Stone's men gave the same in return, letting off round after whizzing round from their own pistols and revolvers.

Sarah snuck a peek over the car door she was kneeling behind and saw Sergeant Mattock. He was aiming shots carefully, not, as yet, lining up kill shots, seemingly more interested in suppressing the enemy than killing him. It was a stupid tactic and not something Mattock would not do ignorantly. Ollie was blind-firing around the back of one of the vans, squeezing his eyes shut in fear as he pulled the trigger on a shiny revolver. He might not have been the solider the rest of the men were, but he was keeping his ground all the same. Rat was an entirely different animal. He was smiling gleefully as he unloaded round upon round into one of the MCU's black Range Rovers. Spots and the older man, Graves, had similar expressions on their faces, but her father's final man, Rupert, was completely blank, returning fire like a robot and showing no emotion of any kind. Sarah had seen men like him before, the ones who entered a daze under fire and let their training take complete charge of their actions. A pure soldier — not good, not evil, just thoroughly trained to do a job.

"Sarah, take the blighters out," her father shouted at her from the other side of the car, bellowing through the open interior.

Sarah looked at the Mac-10 in her hands and realised she was in a firefight. She couldn't stay in cover while her comrades took heavy fire. She was going to have to get involved. It was time to commit herself to her new family. She leapt up and pulled the trigger.

Mattock didn't see her until it was too late.

-14-

Summer, 1987

"Sarah, dinner in one hour."

Eight-year-old Sarah ran through the living room and into the kitchen where her mother stood in front of the stove. The air was hot, from both the bright sunlight coming through the window and from the heat coming from the cottage's Aga. They had lived there less than a year, after having decided to lay down roots, instead of moving all over the world with her daddy. Sarah loved her new home and had even made a friend at school. Her name was Holly and her parents were farmers. Sometimes, Sarah even got to spend time with her daddy, who was home at the moment for two whole weeks. Her daddy was a brave soldier.

"Can I go out and play until it's ready?" Sarah asked her mother.

"Of course, but don't wander off into the road. Stay by the house."

"Can I have a biscuit to take out with me?"

Her mother turned away from the bubbling pot on the stove and looked at her daughter. She rolled her eyes. "Go on, then. But only one."

Sarah hopped up in the air and then ran over to the biscuit tin, taking out her favourite chocolate digestive. She took a bite immediately but took the rest out into the sunshine with her. She decided to play beside the house, in the pebbled driveway that was flat enough for her to kick her football around. Her father was always on at her about how little girls should not be interested in playing football, but she loved running around and kicking it far more than playing with her dolls or the plastic kitchen she had got for Christmas.

Her daddy was in the garage, where she was not to disturb him. She often heard him talking in there on the phone he had at the back, inside a little office, but she never understood what he was saying. He spoke lots about places with funny names and about men that sounded scary. She always stayed away from the garage.

Her daddy's car was parked out on the drive, where it always was when he was home. When he was gone it would sit under a big blanket in the garage. It was really long and a shiny red and looked lots of fun to drive in, but she had never been allowed to go with her father when he drove it. Sometimes her mother was allowed to sit in the passenger seat, but never Sarah. Sometimes, when her father wasn't looking, she would run her hands over it and enjoy the feel of the cold metal.

The lure of the car called to Sarah now and she crept towards it, marvelling at the shafts of light that bounced of its long, round nose. It was a Jagwa and worth lots of money. One day, when she was grown, Sarah was going to own a Jagwa, too. She took another bite of her biscuit and then placed her hands along the bonnet, slowly sliding her fingertips along the bodywork. The hood was made of fabric and could be pulled down in the sunshine, but right now it was up. She ran her fingers along the rough material and found it extremely soft and supple compared to the stiffness of the bodywork. She wondered what it would be like to ride along with the top down, visiting the seaside and seeing the seagulls overhead.

"Sarah!"

Sarah flinched so badly that she tripped and fell backwards. A shard of pebble bit into her palm and made her cry out. Her father appeared, towering over her, and dragged her back up to her feet. "Look what you've done," he shouted while shoving her head in the direction of the car.

She was already in tears, but she was able to see what she had done. On the roof of her daddy's Jagwa was a chocolaty handprint. Her whole body shook in fear, and she wet herself when she realised what was to come.

"Look at you, you stupid girl. You've pissed yourself." Her daddy's hand struck the back of her legs, making her scream. He hit her two more times before he let her go. By that time, her mother had exited the cottage and was standing on the drive.

"What's happened?" she said meekly.

Sarah's father growled. "The little brat covered my car in chocolate."

"Don't be so hard on her. She's a child."

"Get her out of my sight. If I see her again tonight I'm leaving. Do you know how little time I get to myself? Do you know what I do for this country and this family?"

Sarah's mother said nothing, as she rarely did. She just shot her husband a hateful stare and pulled her sobbing daughter in close. A year later she divorced Sarah's father and they went to live in a cramped flat in the city by themselves. Sarah never missed that old cottage even once. And she missed her father even less.

-15-

Mattock took the bullet without fuss, as was his manner. Howard had watched in horror when Sarah leapt up out of cover and fired off a spray of bullets, sending Mattock reeling to the ground, hit and bleeding.

"We have to get out there and help," said Howard. He and Jessica were sitting inside the rearmost of the three black Range Rovers, doing nothing. Mattock had insisted that he and his team secure the perimeter before Howard and Jessica went in to retrieve Krenshaw and Sarah, but when they arrived in the area, the scout team observed Major Stone and his men gearing up to leave. Going in quiet was no longer an option. They had eyes on Krenshaw, out in the open, and he was attempting to flee. Palu gave Mattock the okay and Howard and Jessica were demoted to spectators. Now, Mattock was down, shot by a woman who less than six months ago had fought side-by-side with him.

Howard didn't need to wait for Jessica to agree with him. She was already out of the car and firing off shots across the bonnet, sending a rodent-featured man into hiding. Howard slid across the seats and exited out on the same side, using the long vehicle as sufficient, though imperfect, cover. Major Stone and his men were well-armed, but with handguns and machine pistols. Mattock's team carried recent-issue L85A2 British assault rifles. It was a one-sided affair until Sarah blindsided Mattock.

A leather-skinned, older man popped up from behind the door of one of the black vans and Howard aimed and shot. A spray of red mist erupted from the back of the man's skull and he fell down in a lifeless heap. At the same time, Jessica emptied her magazine and managed to wing a stocky black man in the neck, sending him face first into the open where bullets whizzed over his head. The wounded man screamed for help, begged for it in fact, but was soon shut up. Major Stone leapt out of cover and fired a shot from his hefty pistol, reducing his own man's skull to mush. He was back down in cover before anyone could take a shot at him.

"Give up, Major Stone," shouted Howard. "Two of your men are down and we have you pinned. You'll die here if you don't give yourself up."

The gunfire stopped. Although Mattock was down, his men still numbered seven and were more than happy to keep shooting at fish in barrels, yet they waited now to see if a ceasefire ensued. It didn't appear that Major Stone was going to come out with his hands up, but Howard's words had apparently made the man pause to think.

Howard decided to push the situation. "Do you want your daughter to die, Major Stone? Sarah, I know you can hear me. Mattock's dead. I watched you shoot him when he wasn't looking. Do you really want any more bloodshed? Do you want to shoot me next, or how about Jessica? We were on the same team not so long ago, Sarah. What happened to you?"

There was no answer, so Howard placed his gun down on the bonnet of the Range Rover and stood out from cover, his hands raised above his head.

Jessica grabbed at him but missed. "Howard, what the hell are you doing?"

"Major Stone, I am unarmed, and you are an honourable man. I know you won't shoot me. Come out and talk. Or send your daughter. I'd like to ask her why she just murdered a man who thought very highly of her."

There was more silence and for a moment Howard worried that Major Stone and his people had managed to scurry away some-place, but then he saw the shifting shadows of someone moving behind the torn-up Jaguar. Dr Krenshaw was also still cowering in the background, trying to hide behind a steel wheelie bin.

"Just stop this, Major Stone. It's Dr Krenshaw we want. You needn't have got involved in this."

"Too late now," someone barked in a deep voice that Howard assumed belonged to Major Stone. He hoped he could appeal to the man's honour, or to his daughter's loyalties, but it seemed neither were about to listen.

There was a flash of movement beneath the floodlights.

Something arced into the air, a small black shadow against the glare of the flood lamps. It was followed by three more shadows. Each of them began falling to the ground, right towards Howard and the MCU strike team.

Howard turned and ran, screaming, "Grenades."

-16-

As the MCU strike team leapt for cover, and a series of hellish bangs rocked the air, Major Stone grabbed Dr Krenshaw roughly by the arm and re-opened the warehouse door. Rat and Spots were both uninjured and quickly hurried into the warehouse behind Major Stone. Sarah stood, not knowing which way to go. Did she give herself up to MCU, and face what she had done? Or go after her father and get herself in deeper?

For a moment it seemed like the frightened part of her was going to win out and surrender, but then she thought about her time in the army, the death of her husband and unborn child, and of course the loss of her face. She thought about all the men sent to their deaths on missions they barely understood, and thought about all of the success the MCU had gained off the back of her efforts. She was tired of being used by others, only to be spat out. Her father would be no different, but at least he could get her out of the country. Choosing to follow her father offered the chance at a new life. Giving herself up to the MCU offered a return to her old one.

What made up her mind was Ollie. He'd stopped to wait for her by the door, looking afraid, yet determined. Sarah bolted inside the warehouse with him and caught up with the other men.

Her father glanced at her and seemed like he was about to smile, but he quickly killed the expression before it had chance to take on life. Rat was less happy to see her and snarled and bared his teeth. “Shouldn’t you be back there with your boyfriend? He seemed to know you pretty good.”

“Yeah,” said Spots, speaking to her for the first time that day. “If you’ve set us up I’ll gut you.”

“Agent Hopkins doesn’t know me at all,” she spat back at them. “If he did then he would be running the other way, same as the both of you should do.”

Rat smirked and resumed his hurried march forward.

Spots, however, gave her a brief smirk and seemed to reconsider his position. “Just like your father.”

Ollie came up on her back, grabbed her elbow lightly. Their running had turned into a determined march. “What a mess. How the hell did the MCU know how to find us?”

Sarah looked at him in surprise. “You mean you don’t think I had anything to do with it?”

“If you sold us out to the MCU you would be with them now, wouldn’t you? Instead you took a shot at one of them and escaped.”

Sarah thought about how she had opened fire on Mattock and quickly shook the image from her mind. She liked the cockney hard man a lot and was ashamed at what she’d done. But done it she had and there was no chance to change it now. She needed to get the hell out of there.

Her father led them through to the opposite side of the warehouse, and once there he opened up what would once have been the public entrance to the street. A solitary vehicle sat in the small car park outside: a banged-up, 90s era BMW. He unlocked the vehicle and told them all to get in. Rat sat up front, while Ollie, Sarah, Spots, and Krenshaw wedged themselves uncomfortably into the back. The interior stunk of sweat and cigarettes and the roof cloth was ripped and hanging.

Spots had Krenshaw on his lap, still clutching his briefcase like a life preserver. Ollie sat on one side, while Sarah sat on the other. Major Stone started the engine and they took off, pretty powerfully for such an old car.

"Always good to have a few old bangers in reserve around the city," her father said as though he were trying to teach a lesson. "Never know when you're going to need an alternative escape plan."

Rat was hooting with laughter in the front seat and checking the magazine on his cumbrous Desert Eagle. A gun as powerful as his cock was probably small, Sarah assumed. Spots sat almost sideways on the seat in order to keep hold of Krenshaw and it made it hard for Sarah to see Ollie on the opposite side of the car. Sarah managed to glance over at him through the tangle of limbs and heads. "You okay, Ollie?"

He smiled at her. "I'm fine, just not a natural when it comes to the nasty stuff. I'll be okay."

"You look like you're about to shit yourself," Spots muttered.

"It's just adrenaline," said Krenshaw, a little calmer now as time passed. "It will where off."

Sarah sneered. "Wow, did you learn that at medical school? Or at nursery when the teacher told you not to get over-excited?"

Krenshaw looked at her like one of his diseases, something to be studied and handled carefully, yet that did not stop him from talking to her with a voice dripping with disdain. "I find that stating the obvious to a patient is more comforting than explaining the complex. I was merely trying to be help calm your colleague down. You're rather rude."

"Compassion, huh? That's an odd emotion for a terrorist. Did you show compassion for the people you infected in Reading? Or South Africa?"

The doctor seemed confused. "I'm sorry, South Africa?"

"Heads down," shouted Major Stone. "Plods up ahead."

They all ducked down until they were told they had the all clear again. When Sarah looked out of the window, she saw that they were leaving Shepard's Bush, most of the way, already, to Heathrow.

"How will we get through airport security?" she asked her father. "MCU will have posted an alert to every airport in the country."

"Of course they will, but we're not going to be travelling as ourselves. Our false passports will get us out of the country without issue."

Sarah couldn't see how it was possible for a group of fugitives to move through an airport unmolested, but she had no option but to follow her father's lead. She glanced sideways at Krenshaw and felt revolted.

"How can you be so calm?" she asked the doctor. "You're wanted for the death of dozens of people."

He grinned. "Oh, I assure you that the number will exceed mere dozens when my virus takes its full course. Did you get to see my work in Reading? It was quite beautiful, don't you think? The West is slow to appreciate the rest of the world's suffering, but I did them the favour of speeding up the virus's infection rate and lethality. Whiteknight Hospital will be littered with the dead before the week's end. Maybe then, Westminster and the rest of Europe will actually start taking notice of what the 3rd World has had to endure for decades. Perhaps some of the money this country spends on mind-numbing television, to forget the World's suffering, will go where it is actually needed. Do you know that the NHS spends three-million-pounds per year on unnecessary plastic surgery? This country would rather throw money at plastic tits than a Congolese orphanage full of dying children. It spends sixteen-million a year on obesity. Can you believe it? All that money going to gluttons while nearly eight-hundred-and-seventy million people starve worldwide. It is time they took notice. Unfortunately, they will not do that until their charmed lives are endangered."

Sarah shook her head in disbelief. "You actually think you're one of the good guys, don't you?"

"History is full of martyrs. Even Jesus was hated in his time."

Ollie chuckled. "Talk about a deity complex. I suppose you think you'll live forever?"

"Alas, no. My AIDS is quite severe and I doubt I'll make another year."

Sarah flinched. "You have AIDS?"

"Get the fuck away from me," said Spots, trying to shove the doctor off his lap.

Krenshaw's demeanour changed and he spat his next words with venom. "You see? The way you all flinch proves my point about the stigma and disregard the West holds for Africa's suffering. I am, in actual fact, not infected with AIDS but dying of throat cancer — something you can't catch, so calm yourselves. My mission was decided upon, however, not for my own health concerns but for the poor people of Sub-Saharan Africa and beyond. When I watched a child of five die of untreated bronchitis, I decided that the human race was failing. No one mourned this five-year old girl, you see, for her parents had both already died of other untreated conditions. Her body lay in the dirt for hours, passers-by looking through her as though she did not even exist, until I took her in my arms and buried her in a field. I never knew her name and no one will ever know where she was buried. Her life was deemed no more important than that of a mayfly, and so I deemed the life of those who failed to help her no more significant than a mayfly. My revenge is a revenge you have wrought upon yourselves, and when I am no more, buried in some field the same way that nameless girl was, there will be hope and promise in the world again. Nothing unites humanity like fear. Let the whole world fear AIDS, Ebola, and every other 3rd World bogeyman. Perhaps then, we can find compassion that reaches beyond our own selfish borders."

The sun was coming up and Sarah blinked her eyes. She had nothing else to say to Krenshaw, for as much as she found him abhorrent, she understood the power of violence and intimidation to attain one's goals. What the doctor was suggesting might just have worked, too, if he'd been able to continue, but there was no part of what he was doing that was in any way right. As much as the world was off-kilter, there were people who cared about the plight of the 3rd World and Sarah was sure the number would grow of its own accord, without having to be beaten into compassion. Better to give willingly, she thought, than to have one's charitable arm thrust out forcefully.

They pulled into Heathrow airport ten-minutes later and finally got out of the cramped BMW. They straightened their backs and moaned with relief. Her father went around to the boot and put on a smart woollen overcoat and pulled up the collar. The rest of them had to face the cold morning in what they were wearing. When they got going, her father didn't bother locking the car, for they would not be going back to it, he told them.

"You did well," her father said to her as they walked towards the terminal.

"You killed Rupert," was all she said in reply, having wanted to bring it up the whole time in the car. "Your own man."

"He was dying. Even if he wasn't, he wouldn't have wanted to be captured."

Sarah huffed. "Captured. You speak like we're at war."

"We are. Maybe if you had continued to serve, you would have seen it more clearly. Was the needless bloodshed not clear to you when a British missile killed your husband? Thomas, wasn't it? What a crime he committed, being in the wrong place at the wrong time. I'm sure our government owned up to their crimes profusely. Made amends?"

Sarah shook her head. "They swept it under the rug."

"Of course they did, as they have with uncountable other vile acts before and after. If only you'd seen the things my men have seen, Sarah. Believe me, Graves and Rupert were ready to die for the mission. I did only what I would ask for myself. I would rather die than be brought in by this government's vipers."

"MCU aren't like that," she said. "They're good people trying to help. I know."

"Then perhaps you shouldn't have shot one of them. They might have had you back. Nice shot, by the way."

Sarah frowned. "What do you mean?"

"You winged my old sergeant. Barely even touched him to be honest. The Sergeant Mattock I knew would have carried on fighting, but perhaps he's not quite as tough as he used to be."

Sarah had deliberately aimed at Mattock's hip, not wanting to deliver a kill wound and not wanting to risk a ricocheting round in his centre mass. She had spread her shots wide, yet grazed Mattock a little deeper than she'd meant to. The shock had turned his lights out and left him looking dead. When Howard had spoken out to her, he obviously thought as much, but there was no way she was going to kill Mattock. He was a good man. But shooting him was bad enough for her not to want to remain in the UK a moment longer than she had to.

Major Stone had them all spread out as they entered Terminal 1. They would be suspicious as a group, so were ordered to check in separately, before gathering back as strangers at the departure gate. Their guns were all left back in the car, a treasure trove for a would-be thief and impossible to get through security. Sarah and her father took charge of Krenshaw and headed off, while Rat, Spots and Ollie split off. As most major airports usually were, Heathrow was teeming with people. It was a place without circadian rhythms — no day, no night, always busy. Airports held a lot in common with Casinos in that respect and they both had the same depressing air of exhaustion and weariness.

Sarah stood beneath the passenger information screens and scanned for her flight details. Her father nudged her and told her not to bother. "We three aren't checking in as civilians. This way."

Sarah followed after her father, making sure Krenshaw stayed close by. She was still surprised by the doctor's compliance and astounded that he seemed in no way concerned. In fact, he seemed a little excited as they headed towards a security checkpoint at the far end of the check-in desks.

Her father pulled a small pouch the size of an old VHS tape and a shiny document from his coat pocket and handed it over to the unsmiling gate officer. Sarah noticed that the small pouch was stamped with the words: DIPLOMATIC BAG. The same thing was printed on Krenshaw's briefcase, she noticed.

Sarah was impressed when the three of them were ushered through without so much as a cursory inspection, and even Krenshaw's briefcase passed without scrutiny. The only think that got even the slightest look were the grotesque scars on her face, but that she was used to.

"We're all travelling under diplomatic papers," her father explained a moment later. "Our official business states we are in charge of a doctor and dangerous samples needed immediately by the World Health Organisation."

"In Libya?" asked Sarah.

Her father shrugged. "It won't need to pass deeper inspection. We're already through."

"How did you get diplomatic designation?"

"High friends in high places. The people I am working for have a great deal of clout."

"So why do they need someone like you? You're just a thug."

The comment earned a scolding glance and her father's emerald eyes drilled into her as he spoke. "Great minds don't always have great stomachs. A driver might steer a car, but he will go nowhere without tyres on the ground. I am a tyre. I carry the drivers of this world where they need to go, and if anything gets in my way, I roll right over it."

"I thought you were done taking orders?"

"I'm done being expendable and I'm done following orders I don't agree with."

"You still sound expendable to me," she said, not sure why she was so intent on harassing her father. "Tyres get replaced. I would much rather be the driver. The driver is in control of the tyres and they go wherever he wants them to, until they wear out or burst."

Her father's ruddy cheeks quivered.

"I think," Krenshaw interrupted, "that Major Stone merely used a flawed analogy. Truthfully, he is more like a syringe; surgically precise with the ability to penetrate while barely being noticed. While doctors may think themselves gods, it is the unassuming syringe that makes things happen."

Major Stone nodded at Krenshaw in what seemed to be thanks.

Sarah cursed. "What the hell is going on here? Why is our hostage jumping to your defence? And why does he seem so perfectly content to be in our custody?"

"Because he knows what's good for him," said her father flatly.

"How? South Africa will be far less gentle than we are."

"Trust me, daughter. I know what I am doing and Krenshaw understands his role. Everything is going as intended."

Sarah glanced at Krenshaw who seemed to be smiling, if a little confused by the conversation. Her father was looking at her now in a way far softer than she was used to, and it crumbled her resolve. He seemed to be asking her to trust him, which was something he never would have cared about in the past.

She grunted, flapped her arms in defeat. "Not like I can turn back now, is it?"

"Good. Let's go and get eyes on Rat and the others, then we can kick our heels for an hour until the flight."

They headed into a wide eating area and sat down at an open plan cafe, ordering some drinks and snacks from the tired-looking waitress. There, they were eventually joined by Ollie, Spots, and Rat. Rat, as usual, sneered at her on sight. Ollie was far gentler and gave her a pat on the back where she was sitting alone in the corner.

"Everything go okay?" he asked her.

She nodded. "Yeah. Too easy, in fact."

"That's what's so great about your father; he makes tough work seem like nothing."

Sarah studied Ollie as he sat down opposite her. There was something very comforting about his face, maybe even something familiar. He was a soft man doing hard work, and he didn't wear it well. "I don't get you," she said. "How did a man like you ever end up with a man like my father?"

"Obligation."

"Why are you obligated to my father?"

Ollie seemed put off for a second, as if he had spoken without thinking. It became obvious when he tried to backtrack. "He's... allowing me to make amends for what happened. My wife."

Sarah nodded. "I don't believe that's all of it. You're not a violent man — not by choice, anyway. My father rallied you to his cause, made you take up arms, but how did he do it? How did he even find you?"

Ollie sighed. "I've known your father a long time, Sarah, although he pretty much disappeared off the face of the earth when he joined the army. We grew up together as kids, me a few years older. Even back then, your father was tough. At school he would keep the bullies off me, even thought he was younger, even when they towered over him. He was my little bodyguard. It wasn't because he loved me — I'm not sure he's ever loved anyone." He looked at her then and realised what he's said. "Sorry. It was because of his sense of duty that he protected me, and his sense of duty is unbreakable."

"Why did my father feel a sense of duty to you?" she urged.

Ollie began fiddling with his fingers and looking down at the wedding ring he still wore. "Your father never met my wife. We had already lost touch long before then, but when he found out she had died, he came immediately to visit me in Sri Lanka — again, probably because he felt a duty to do so. I found out that he had been in Sri Lanka a few times before, helping the government fight the Tamil Tigers, and he told me that he had once even looked in on me. He had seen how happy I was and felt his duty to me was complete, which was why he never reached out to me. His life and my life were too different to gel comfortably, so he stayed away. But when Darla was killed he had to come and make sure I was okay."

"I still don't understand," said Sarah. "I never heard him speak about you once. Who are you to my father?"

Ollie shook his head and exhaled slowly, before looking at her and saying, "I'm your father's brother, Sarah; your uncle. My wife was your auntie and the four-year-old son I had snatched away in the attack on my school was your cousin."

Sarah reeled back in her chair. As a young woman she'd had no one. Her mother died young and her father had shown no interest, yet all this time she had had a kindly uncle, a man who had now been turned to killing upon her father's influence. She floundered for a moment. "I...why didn't you ever...I..."

Ollie shrugged. "I didn't know you existed until six months ago. Your father and I had gone so long without contact that I grew old in the time since you were born. I'm sorry I kept it from you, but your father..."

Sarah nodded. She understood very well how her father had a way of making people dance to his tune, even if he was playing nothing but wrong notes. "It's okay," she said. "I'm glad I know."

"Okay, men," said her father almost half-an-hour later. "The plane is boarding, so let's move."

Everyone finished their drinks and got up. When they began heading towards the gate, Sarah noticed that Krenshaw had forgotten his briefcase. He'd left it beneath one of the tables. She headed back to get it.

"Leave it, Sarah," her father shouted.

Sarah pulled her hand away from the briefcase and frowned. "Why?"

"Because it's set to go off."

-17-

When Mattock sat up minutes after the attack, swearing and shouting, Howard almost wept. The man was part of his family and, while they may not always agree, there was a mutual respect between the two of them, as there was between all members of the MCU, which was what made Sarah's actions extra sickening.

"She'll pay for this," Howard growled as he knelt beside Mattock. The grenades had made short work of the three MCU Range Rovers and Major Stone and his people had got away; but no one was seriously hurt and that was the important thing. The only people to die were two of Major Stone's men. Men they were currently in the process of IDing.

Mattock gritted his teeth, pulled up his shirt and protective vest, and examined the damage. Blood was everywhere and Howard felt himself growing ever more furious at what his former colleague had down, but Mattock just ended up chuckling.

"Just a flesh wound," he said. His hands were covered in fresh red blood but he seemed entirely composed. "I'm bloody embarrassed for passing out like some pansy. She barely hit me."

"We have a team on the way," said Jessica. "We'll get you back to the Earthworm where I can take a proper look at you."

"I'm fine, luv." Mattock managed to climb to his feet, barely wincing. "Just point me in the right direction and I'm dandy."

Howard placed a hand on the man's shoulder. "I've got this now. Wherever Sarah and her father have gone with Krenshaw, I'll be the one to find them."

"Go easy on Sarah," said Mattock.

"Why? She shot you."

"If that bird had wanted me dead, I would be, mate. She shot to wound – barely at that. She's not too far gone. Reach out to her."

Howard thought about things for a minute. He'd seen Sarah shoot a gun before and it was true she knew what she was doing. There was little chance she would've missed the mark with a full magazine from a machine pistol. Perhaps she had intended merely to graze Mattock, but she still helped Krenshaw escape. After what he had witnessed at Whiteknight Hospital, that was unforgivable.

"Hey, I've got something over here."

Howard looked around to see one of the strike team members, a young blond guy called Wilder, shouting him over. At the man's feet was the body of an elderly gentleman, looking much frailer in death than he had in life only an hour before.

"What do you have?" Howard asked the young officer.

"I found these." Wilder handed over what he had, then said, "Oh, that I had wings like a dove! I would fly away and be at rest."

"I'm sorry, what?"

"It's from the bible. Seems like Major Stone and his people are planning on flying."

Howard frowned, then took the passport and ticket from the strange young man and ran his eyes over them. The name on the documents would probably be false, but the destination was Libya. It was it pretty obvious Major Stone planned on getting out of the country.

"Can I leave you with this?" he asked Jessica, meaning the mess that was the three disabled Range Rovers and a handful of disorientated MCU agents.

"Yes, of course, but where are you going?"

Howard showed her the tickets. "There's no way I'm letting Krenshaw leave this country. I'll shoot him if I have to. They could still be heading for Heathrow."

Jessica sighed. "Wait for backup, Howard."

"Backup is here, licking its wounds." Mattock glared but Howard continued. "Major Stone's flight leaves in less than an hour. Someone needs to go, right now. It will take too long to assemble another team and make a plan."

"Then have Palu ground all flights to buy us time."

"We do that and Major Stone goes to ground. Our best chance is to pin him down at the airport where he can't escape, but I need to move now."

Jessica nodded slowly, knowing him well enough not to bother arguing. "Then go," she said. "But bloody be careful."

Howard put a call in to Mandy, MCU's most skilled driver, and told him he needed to get to the airport quickly. Ten minutes later, he was picked up by a sleek black Jaguar. Mandy spoke little, so Howard stated his destination. "Get me to Heathrow."

-18-

Mandy dropped Howard right outside the entrance to Terminal 1. Howard wasted no time rushing inside. He flashed his badge at airport security and was let through the check-in barriers without question. Palu had called ahead and airport security were ready and waiting to help in whatever ways it could. The leader of the security force was a short man named Tariq Riaz.

"What do you need from my team?" asked Tariq obligingly.

Howard told him. "I need a radio that I can reach you on. We are looking for a small group of men, and a woman with a badly scarred face."

"Should be easy enough to find. Here, take my radio. Set it to 'wide' and you'll broadcast to every member of the team. There are over a hundred of us in total, more than enough to handle whatever you need."

"Good. I don't want anyone getting hurt, so I'm going to try and get a view of the targets before deciding how to proceed. I'll head to the gate and see if I can get eyes on, but if your men spot the targets first I want to know right away."

Tariq nodded. "Of course. Is it true that one of the men you're after is responsible for the Ebola epidemic in Reading?"

"How did you know that?"

"The news. I just got an update about a firefight in Watford involving MCU and a man suspected for the Reading outbreak. Now, here you are, another MCU agent, chasing down a group of dangerous men."

The local police must have arrived on scene after Howard had left Mattock, Jessica, and the others. Once the local police got wind of anything, it went straight to the attention of the press.

Howard smiled. "You're smart. That's good. And you're correct, one of the men is responsible for Ebola Reading. He is extremely dangerous, so help me catch the sonofabitch."

"I'll do whatever you need me to," said Tariq.

Howard rushed off towards the appropriate departure gate, staying close to the walls and trying to merge with the various groups travelling. It was difficult to blend in with the various families, businessmen, and lovers on route to exotic destinations. He was the only one not wearing sandals and t-shirt, or formal business attire; not to mention that those travelling to Libya specifically wore the traditional gowns of that country. Howard stuck out like a sore thumb in his cheap suit and tie. He decided to roll up his sleeves, ditch the tie, and unbutton his collar. He also took the time to quickly purchase a baseball cap from one of the stores. It wasn't a perfect disguise, but it didn't need to be.

A ringing sound made him flinch and he realised it was his mobsat. He answered the call and it was Palu.

"Howard, the remainder of Mattock's team are finishing up with the local police and will be on your location in twenty. Can you hold things that long?"

"No. The flight to Libya leaves in twenty minutes. I have airport security helping me, so I will have to bring the targets in myself."

Palu breathed down the phone. "Okay. Are you armed?"

"Yes."

"I suspect Major Stone will be also."

"How would he get a gun through check-in?"

"Diplomatic papers. The entire team here at the Earthworm is working the Intel, and as part of that we ran every single check-in confirmed through Heathrow in the last hour. Three people were passed through as diplomats. Two men and a woman. When one of the analysts called up to confirm details, the officer in charge described the female in the group as 'a freak'. Upon elaboration he said that her face was badly scarred."

Howard exhaled. "Sarah. Pretty hard to hide with wounds like hers."

"If they got through with diplomatic bags they could be in possession of anything. Be careful. We've been getting more Intel that tells us Major Stone has been behind several recent attacks against UK assets abroad. I'm not sure he's simply gone rogue. I think he's turned against us entirely."

"Is there anyway Sarah doesn't know what her father is doing?"

Palu breathed down the phone again. "I don't see how. She engaged in a firefight with Mattock's men and helped Dr Krenshaw escape. We both know that Sarah has a grudge against this country. Her father might have convinced her to join his cause under the mutual flag of disenchantment."

"I still don't know what Major Stone's cause even is."

"I think it has something to do with Syria," said Palu. "I still have analysts working the angles, but Major Stone went rogue during a mission in Syria to take out an ISIS arms cache. He successfully found the site and lased it for an airstrike but never returned radio communication after the bombs dropped. Command assumed he and his team were lost, but they popped up a month later and assassinated that ISIS leader. Just be careful, Howard. Major Stone is one of the deadliest men this country has ever had at its disposal, and somehow we pissed him off."

"His daughter, too," said Howard. "I'll call in when I have something."

"Roger that."

Howard got moving again. He was approaching an eating area, surrounded by cafes and fast food chains on both sides. It was then that he saw Sarah sitting and drinking coffee. He had to suppress the urge to draw his gun right then and there, but it would have been the wrong move. With Krenshaw, Major Stone, and the other men, Sarah's group equalled six — all of them deadly.

Howard grabbed the radio Tariq had given him and called it in. "All targets located in," he looked around for a landmark, "area between Lorraine's Bistro and Lanier's Italian Cafe."

"Sending a team to you now," came Tariq's reply. "Over."

"Roger that." Howard moved into the doorway of a small amusement arcade and peered around the edge of the wall next to a fruit machine. There were people all around and the last thing he wanted to do was test the theory that Major Stone was carrying a weapon. The targets were all finishing their drinks and preparing to get up, though. The call had been made for their flight and they were able to board. That could not happen. If Major Stone made it onto the plane, he had the option of taking the pilot hostage and forcing a take-off. A man of Major Stone's abilities could drop himself down in the middle of the Sahara and disappear with the winds.

While Howard was still deciding what to do, Sarah broke off from the departing group and travelled back towards the cafe. For a moment, Howard thought she had spotted him, but he soon realised that she had forgotten something. Sarah bent down to pick up a briefcase from beneath one of the tables but recoiled when he farther shouted at her.

Howard heard the words exactly as Major Stone said them: "It's set to go off."

Howard had no choice anymore. He stepped out from cover and pointed his gun. "MCU, freeze!"

-19-

"MCU, freeze!"

Sarah dove down behind the coffee counter while her father and his men dropped down into cover behind various upturned tables. Meanwhile, several hundred innocent travellers started a stampede at the sight of Howard's gun. Like frightened antelope they ran and leapt for cover and filled the air with their terrified screams. Sarah stood amongst the flowing river of people and felt lost, confused. The fact that Howard had managed to relocate her and her father was a shock, but it was probably inevitable since they'd been forced to flee so suddenly from the warehouse. Carefully laid plans were the ones that left most clues when gone awry.

"Sarah, get down on the floor," shouted Howard. "There's only two ways out of this airport, dead or alive, and unlike you I don't enjoy shooting former colleagues."

Sarah scurried from her hiding place over to where her father was hiding behind a table. Howard could probably have drawn a bead on her then, but she had counted on him not wanting to pull the trigger just yet and she was right. He didn't fire and she made it over to her father in one piece. Major Stone was unzipping the diplomatic pouch he'd been carrying in his coat pocket. Sarah was flabbergasted when he pulled out two pieces of a handgun, as well as a loaded magazine. He slid the detached barrel onto the handgun's frame and slapped the magazine into the bottom of the grip. It was a small gun, a bright silver Ruger.

"This is madness," Sarah told her father.

"This is war," he said. "There's no distinction between madness and sanity, only what's necessary. We need to get that briefcase."

"Why, what's in it?"

"Krenshaw's lifework, and it's going to go off right in our faces if we don't get it and reset the timer."

Howard shouted at them again. "Major Stone, Sarah, give yourselves up. None of you are getting away."

Sarah glanced around between the upturned tables and spotted Ollie — her Uncle — crouching next to Rat and Spots. Ollie gave her a sad look that suggested he regretted the situation as much as she did. They had crossed a line and neither could see a way back.

Krenshaw made a break for it. The skinny doctor raced across the cafe floor, heading for his briefcase, but stopped short and spun as a bullet struck his chest. He collapsed onto one of the tables and lay still.

There was more panic as the innocent bystanders abandoned their hiding places and broke for greater safety. The gun shot had been like a starting pistol and now they were all off their lines and running for their lives.

"This is the final warning," Howard bellowed in a voice more commanding than Sarah remembered. "Come out, hands up and empty. This ends now."

Major Stone leapt up and took a shot at Howard, missing the target by a hairsbreadth. The bullet lodged in the concrete of the wall and sent Howard leaping back into cover.

It was then that Airport security guards surrounded the area. Each carried a Heckler & Koch MP5s. Enough firepower to rip a man to confetti.

Sarah went to put her hands in the air and surrender, but her father grabbed her shoulder and yanked her back down. "Don't disappoint me," he said to her, with a pulsing rage in his emerald eyes.

"We're done for," she said. "This is a colossal screw-up. I don't know what I'm even doing here with you. You never gave a damn about me and I followed you into Hell anyway. I'm an idiot."

"You are my daughter," he said. "And we will make it out of this, I promise you. You're one of my men now and I don't intend on seeing you die until you're ready."

Sarah shook her head. "You never made a single promise to me that you kept. You've been helping Krenshaw all along, haven't you? We didn't capture him, we rescued him."

"Krenshaw is a means to an end. His work is what matters. My mission is to make sure that what is inside that briefcase serves its purpose."

"What purpose?"

There was more gunfire and Sarah flinched, before carefully peering over an upturned table. To her utter surprise, Rat had managed to get the jump on one of the airport security guards and had taken his weapon, which he quickly turned on the rightful owner and two of his colleagues. Spots was quick to scurry over and grab one of the dead men's fallen MP5s and join the firefight.

The air filled with the sound of a dozen jackhammers.

Sarah's father beamed, the first time she'd ever seen such an expression from him. "See?" he said. "There is no situation my men can't handle."

"We're outnumbered five to one," she said.

"Exactly, they won't know what hit them."

Sarah's father leapt up and expended what was left of his handgun's ammo and sent a handful of guards into cover. It bought enough time for Spots to pick up another fallen MP5 and toss it to him. He caught the weapon easily and fired off a stream of rounds in one smooth motion, taking out another guard. The rest of the airport's vanguard visibly shrank as they realised they were losing men fast. Rat's assault had been quick and brutal, rocking their confidence and keeping them from advancing. Now, barely a single one of them dared to break cover.

Sarah stayed where she was. Things had got completely out of hand. She had just wanted to flee the country, start again. She had never wanted this, never wanted to fight her own country. As much as she hated what her government represented, she bore no malice to the people who fought under its banner. They were innocent cogs, like she had once been.

Finally, she broke cover, but not to fight. Instead, she hurried towards the briefcase, intending to stop whatever was inside of it from getting out. Was it Ebola, or something worse? The thought of something invisible yet deadly made her skin crawl. She wasn't trained to fight something she couldn't see. Put a man in front of her and she could pull the trigger, but a virus...

Whistling, snapping gunfire continued overhead as Sarah crawled along on her belly. She heard wounded men cry out in pain but was sure none of them were her father's men. Rat, Spots, and Major Stone were ex-SAS and could eat airport security guards for breakfast, as they were doing now — but they couldn't fight forever. This was a suicide mission. How had her father changed so much? What had happened to him to make him disregard his life?

She was just about to grab the briefcase, and could even hear something inside ticking, when a hefty boot caught her in the ribs.

"What are you doing, sweetheart?" Rat appeared in her view and kicked her hard again in the stomach. He fired off a few rounds from the two MP5s he was now holding akimbo, before ducking down into cover beside Sarah and grinning in her face.

Sarah tried to catch her breath but Rat punched her in the mouth and sent her into a daze.

"Told you I was going to get some payback, you ugly bitch," he said in the raspy tones of a predator.

"My...my father will kill you."

"Maybe, or maybe he won't give two shits. Way I see it, we're all dead anyway. The only thing that makes our lives mean anything is what's inside that briefcase. What do you plan on doing with it?"

Sarah winced and tried to catch her breath. "I plan on stopping it going off."

Rat laughed. "Good luck with that. I don't think it has an 'off' switch. You do, though." He prodded her mouth with the muzzle of one of the MP5s. The hot metal burned her lips, and then her tongue as Rat forced it between her teeth. "Say goodnight, sweetheart."

"Goodnight."

Rat's head exploded and Sarah yelled out in horror as his body toppled sideways.

Ollie looked down at Sarah with that same regretful smile he'd had on his face earlier. "I told you he'd stab you in the back as soon as he was supposed to be watching it. Come on, we have to give ourselves u-"

Ollie flew backwards and landed hard on his back. The colour red immediately began to bloom on his chest.

Sarah slid over to him on her belly. "Shit! Ollie. Ollie, no."

Ollie shook his head, gasped, then managed to talk in a groan. Blood appeared at the corners of his slowly moving mouth. "I knew about...the briefcase. I know and it's...wrong. You need to stop your father, Sarah. Darla, she would be...s-s-so ashamed."

"Shush," said Sarah, but Ollie was already dead. She didn't kiss him or weep, she had barely known the man; perhaps that was the biggest tragedy of all. There was still time to make it right, though. If Sarah had never got involved in any of this, then her father and Krenshaw would have carried out their plan without a hiccup. Her involvement, however, had screwed everything up, and there was still time for her to put a stop to her father's mission.

Sarah turned away from Ollie and went to go back and grab the briefcase. She had to stop this.

But her father reached it first. Major Stone held the briefcase to his chest and stood up. "Everybody, cease your fire."

His voice was so booming that all of the remaining guards stopped firing immediately. They had lost so many men that they were probably eager for the bullets to stop flying.

Major Stone continued speaking. "I hold in my hands the most deadly disease known to man, engineered by the man responsible for this country's recent Ebola epidemic. My hand is on the release button. If I fall or sleep or get bored, this briefcase will open and the world's most deadly disease will escape. It will kill everybody here, as well as anyone who takes a breath of whatever air escapes into the vents above our heads. It has been engineered to survive almost indefinitely and to multiply quickly within its host. It has been set on a timer, which I have just extended and will continue to do so as long as I am alive. My men-" he looked around and saw Spots was the only one still standing, but he was bleeding badly from a wound in his stomach. His face was pale from massive blood loss. Major Stone exhaled, threw up an arm and casually shot Spots between the eyes with machine gun fire. His body slumped to the floor and Major Stone turned back to his audience. "Correction: my daughter and I are going to leave this airport through whatever back door is closest. Then we will enter a car and drive to safety. Once there, I will arrange for safe disposal of this virus. Do not doubt me, gentlemen, for I am entirely willing to watch this wretched world burn."

Howard stepped out from behind a cracked and crumbling pillar with his gun held up and ready. He was sweating badly. "We can't let you walk out of here, Major Stone. Not going to happen."

Major Stone nodded. "Of course. I understand. Then I suppose none of us will be walking out of here." He raised his MP5 and aimed it at Howard. It should have been enough to provoke a shot from one of the airport's security guards, but they obviously feared the virus too much to pull the trigger. "Would you prefer a bullet, Agent? Or would you like to lose your skin once the virus takes you? I offer you the courtesy of choice because you were once a friend of my daughter."

Howard put a hand up, just to reassert that no one should pull the trigger. "All flights have been grounded, Major. This airport is very easy to contain once it's on lockdown, which it now is. Your super-virus will wither and die right here where we stand."

Major Stone grunted. "Enough deaths to make the news, I assure you — and that is the point, after all. There are powerful men in this world who wish to send a message; and I am their messenger. The death of you and a handful of upstanding airport personnel will suffice, as Pyrrhic a victory as it may be. I am not a man who fails, upon my honour."

Howard lowered his gun and sighed. "What happened, Major? I saw what Krenshaw did to the people at Whiteknight hospital. Why do you want to follow a coward? Why do you want to be associated with a man like him?"

"He and I are not the same, Agent. Count the dead around you. Do I look like a coward?"

Howard looked around at all the dead bodies, men from both sides. "That's how people will remember you if you do this, Major."

"I'm SAS. Men in the SAS don't get to leave legacies. Make of me what you will once I am dead. I couldn't care less."

Sarah saw her father's finger twitch on the trigger, the MP5 still pointed at Howard. If he fired, Howard would die and the security guards would open fire. Then Major Stone's hand would fall from the briefcase and God-knows-what would be released into the confined atmosphere of the airport. She had to do something.

"Stop this, daddy. You're not going to achieve anything, don't you see? I don't want to die."

Her father looked down at her with sadness. "You are pitiful, daughter. Don't you want to die for something important?"

"No," she said. "I want to live for something important."

Major Stone shook his head. He scooped his foot around one of the MP5s that Rat had dropped when he died and kicked it towards her. "Shoot me, then," he said. "You want this to end, then be a man and finish it. Show me you have a cock."

Sarah looked down at the weapon by her leg and went to grab it but couldn't. She couldn't make her hand move towards the MP5, even though she knew that she could end this right now. She had killed men before, but she couldn't kill this one. She couldn't shoot her father.

Major Stone rolled his eyes and looked like he wanted to spit on her. "I wish I'd had a son. To think that Ollie lost a boy of four while you continue to live."

Sarah growled. "I'm not a fucking man, daddy; get over it already. But you're right, I can't shoot you." She leapt up and tackled her father around the legs, lifting him up and throwing him backwards. He fell onto his shoulders, the briefcase flailing in his hand, his MP5 firing at the ceiling. They hit the ground together and Sarah immediately started pummelling her father in the face, smashing his stern cheeks and grizzled chin, glaring into his emerald eyes that matched her own. She beamed and cackled as the blood began to escape Major Stone's mouth. "Doesn't mean I won't kick your arse, though," she screamed at him.

But it was a triumph all too short.

Her father shoved both thumbs into her eyes so hard that Sarah thought he'd blinded her. Then, he brought his legs up and kicked her so hard in the stomach that she felt a rib crack. She fell onto her face, struggling desperately for a breath. Men shouted all around her, but no shots were fired. Though she could barely see, she made out the shape of her father snatching up the briefcase and his MP5 before running away unmolested.

The next thing Sarah knew, men all around her were dragging her harshly to her feet. When her vision finally came back to her in full, she realised that the roughest hands of all belonged to her former partner, Howard. He looked at her like a hated enemy and it made her want to cry.

-20-

Sarah didn't fight back as she was manhandled. Her arms were wrenched behind her back and she was dragged unceremoniously away from the bullet-ridden seating area to a place inside a small amusement arcade. Half of the remaining guards had chased after her father, but the rest stayed behind to clear up the mess Major Stone and his men had left behind.

"I want to speak with her alone," Howard said, marching up to Sarah until his sweating face was right up against hers. He grabbed her roughly by the arm and yanked her away from the two men guarding her.

Sarah couldn't bring herself to look her former colleague in the eye, so she stared down at the floor instead, then, when she spotted a bloodstain on the carpet, she looked at her shoes.

Howard shoved her back against the wall. "What the hell happened to you, Sarah? How did you get involved in all this?"

Sarah couldn't find her voice.

"Talk, Sarah. Believe me, I'm the last person who will be willing to listen."

Sarah forced herself to look up at Howard and felt tears run down the good side of her face. The other side lacked feeling and the ducts rarely opened beneath her left eye. “I didn’t know,” she said. “I...I was abducted, shoved in a cell and kept for four months.”

Howard softened a little, but his folded arms made his hostility clear. “Abducted by whom?”

“My father. I managed to escape a few days ago. I was just about to get away and then...he was there, my father. He was the one who kidnapped me outside of Bradley’s funeral. We got in his way when we took down Hesbani.”

“Hesbani? What are you talking about?”

“Someone paid my father for Hesbani’s head, but we got there first. We cost him a lot of money.”

Howard frowned, kept his arms folded. “What does any of that have to do with any of this? Why were you working with Dr Krenshaw? Do you know what he has done?”

Sarah nodded. “My father said he was taking Krenshaw abroad and handing him over to the South African government for justice. I didn’t know he was going to do any of this, I swear. He dragged me along and, before I knew it, I was fighting the MCU. God, how is Mattock? Is he alright? Tell him I’m sorry. I’m so sorry. I didn’t mean for any of this. I just wanted to get out, start again.”

“Mattock is fine,” said Howard, finally unfolding his arms. “He knows you shot wide on purpose. In fact he told me to go easy on you. Not sure I could be so forgiving if somebody shot me.”

“Howard I-”

Somebody shouted. “Agent Hopkins.”

Howard spun around. An Asian man in a guard’s uniform was hailing him from the cafe area.

Howard grabbed Sarah and took her along. He seemed to know the guard calling him. "Tariq, what is it?"

"We have a survivor."

Sarah's eyes went wide and for a moment she hoped that it was Ollie, but she was soon disappointed when she saw it was Krenshaw. Sarah forgot the situation for a moment, filled and driven by rage. She pushed Howard aside and hurried over to the doctor. Krenshaw was shot in the chest, his breathing ragged, but he was awake for now. The wound was clearly fatal; he did not have long."

"What is in that briefcase?" she demanded. "Tell me."

Despite his obvious pain, Krenshaw managed to smile. "With pleasure." He said, before coughing and spluttering. Blood seeped between his lips, but he managed to continue. "Inside the briefcase is my masterpiece, a disease so deadly it will bring the West to its knees and finally bring the world the equilibrium it needs. There will be no more 3rd World, no more elitism; just mankind's united struggle against a virus more powerful than God. This country is about to become a headless chicken. My mission may have failed, but your father will go on to strike at the heart of this country. It will be an example to the world."

Sarah grabbed the doctor and shook him, making him groan. "What is it? What is the virus and how do we stop it?"

"You don't...stop it. It will burn you from the inside. Your flesh will melt away until there is nothing left but bone and fat. I call it...the Peeling." Krenshaw's body clenched and a mouthful of blood spewed out of his mouth. Sarah tried to hold onto him, but he bucked out of her grasp and spread out on the tiles.

"He's dead," said Howard, pulling her away. "What was he talking about, Sarah? What is your father planning?"

"I have no idea. Something's happened to him. He's not the same."

The security guard, Tariq, looked at Howard and said, "Should I take her into custody? Your director has been on the line, he's sending a team to work with the Home Office in clearing this mess up. Seven of my men are dead and the whole airport is on lockdown."

"I'm sorry," said Howard. "Truly. I know what it's like to lose men, but this women isn't responsible. She wasn't involved in the firefight. She's one of ours."

Tariq raised an eyebrow and looked at Howard with suspicion.

Howard was not deterred. "Sarah's been working undercover for MCU. Her father, Major Stone, is a wanted man and, as his daughter, she was uniquely placed to infiltrate his operation. Now Major Stone's men are dead and we very nearly had him, too. My people from MCU will clear everything up with you, Tariq, but, right now, Sarah and I need to find Major Stone before whatever is inside that briefcase gets out. The airport must be surrounded. There's no way he can get out, surely?"

Sarah glanced at Howard in confusion. What was he doing? He was lying on her behalf, but why?

Tariq stood stiffly for a moment but then shrugged. "You've been given authority here. I can't stop you from doing anything. I'll go find out where Major Stone headed after her fled." The man walked away, speaking into a radio a couple of seconds later.

"Why did you say that?" asked Sarah. "I haven't been helping you."

Howard was still red in the cheeks, but his arms lay by his sides and he no longer glared at her. "Your father is still at large, Sarah. You may still have some use. You are his daughter after all."

"Not sure that will be much help."

"We'll see. Either way, you're going to help me make this right."

Tariq returned a couple of minutes later, shaking his head and blinking slowly. "Your man escaped through a fire exit next to gate 12. He broke a luggage handler's neck on the tarmac and managed to disappear. I don't even know how that's possible. It's broad daylight and there are police officers surrounding the entire airport. Only a ghost could slip away."

"My father was SAS," said Sarah. "He can disappear from a locked room."

Howard took Sarah aside. "You've been working with your father. Where could he be planning to release the virus?"

Something popped into her head and she spoke it before she even understood what it was. "Headless chicken."

Howard looked at her. "What?"

"Krenshaw said the country was about to become a headless chicken, that my father is going to strike at its heart. My father has a grudge against the government for some reason. I think he might attack Breslow."

Howard moaned. "Great. Last year the Queen, this year the Prime Minister. You think he's heading to White Hall, Westminster, Downing Street? Are you sure about this?"

"No, but my father doesn't speak idly. If he's been making comments about the government, it's because he's planning something. Is parliament in session today?"

"I'll find out." Howard turned and made a call on his mobsat, something she remembered doing herself not so long ago. When he turned back again he had a grave expression on his face. "The house is in session all day. They're voting on foreign war policy. Breslow wants to recruit another forty-thousand bodies into the army in order to fight abroad."

Sarah straightened up, hoping she was wrong about her father but pretty much sure. “Infecting an airport with a deadly virus would have been devastating, but wiping out three-hundred MPs will make a good Plan B. We have to stop him.”

Howard nodded. “We will. Nobody else is getting sick because of Krenshaw’s pet projects. Not on my watch.”

“We need to get into the city before my father gets there.”

“Mandy is waiting by. He’ll be glad to see you.”

Sarah couldn’t help but smile. “Is he still a talker?”

“Hasn’t changed a bit.” Howard’s expression had turned briefly jovial, but it now turned quickly serious. “You’re not off the hook for any of this, Sarah. At the moment, the only thing going for you is ignorance and stupidity, but if I find out you knew what your father was planning...”

“I didn’t know,” she said, “but I understand. I really screwed up here, Howard, and all I want to do is make it right. Get me to my father and I’ll finish this, I promise.”

Howard looked at her curiously. “You sure? This is your father we’re dealing with.”

“He’s not my father,” she said. “To be honest, he never has been. Even so, it’s time for me to emancipate myself once and for all.”

-21-

Sarah followed Howard out through the barricade of flashing police cars and headed over to a vehicle she knew well. It was one of the MCU's black Range Rover Westminsters. Howard opened up the rear door and allowed her to hop up inside, while he slid into the front passenger seat beside another man. Sarah spotted Mandy at the wheel and nodded.

"Hey," she said.

Mandy said nothing but nodded back as agreeably as he was able. The thick-necked driver-slash-pilot-slash-stuntman was MCU's mechanical savant. There wasn't a motorised vehicle in the world that Manny Dobbs could not manoeuvre to within the very limits of its capabilities.

"Get us to the Houses of Parliament," said Howard to Mandy. He didn't need to say 'fast' because Mandy went everywhere fast by default. Without word, he gunned the engine and whipped the Range Rover through the police cordon, which stretched for half a mile around the entire airport. Sarah wondered how on earth her father had got away. To lay siege to the country's busiest airport, killing indiscriminately, before disappearing into dust, was a typical feat of the SAS, but Major Stone was no longer a part of their ranks. He was even more dangerous.

The city's traffic was stirred up like a nest of bees, since news obviously spread of the terrorist attack on the airport. After Hesbani last year and the rumours of Ebola Reading being part of a deliberate attack, the residents of the capitol were skittish, afraid. They had every reason to be.

Britain was a country struggling to find a new identity in the world. It was no longer a world power but neither did it fit well into a host of equals. While Europe came together as one, Britain fought desperately to remain empirical, keeping its pound and taking umbrage with any who dared give it orders. After the recent attacks, Britain would be forced to ask for help from the allies it so often spurred. If parliament were hit, then nothing would ever be the same. Sarah wondered if that was what her father wanted. Not just change, but complete renewal.

It took almost an hour to reach Westminster and Howard chatted to Palu constantly via mobsat. Crossing over the bridge towards Big Ben immediately brought back memories for Sarah, memories of Hesbani and her former comrade, Hamish. Had he truly been working for her father all along? Was his hatred for her part of the reason he had turned away from his own country?

"The traffic has held us up badly," said Howard, turning around to face Sarah in the back. "Your father had a head start on us and Palu just got word of a car theft outside of Heathrow ninety-minutes ago. He might have a ride."

Sarah asked, "Does Parliament know it may be a target?"

Howard nodded. "Special Branch is holding a perimeter, but Breslow won't convene. You know her stance on terrorism, she doesn't bend or respond to threats."

Sarah hissed. "Things that don't bend, break."

Mandy skidded up outside the Houses of Parliament and immediately two armed men approached them. Howard hopped out and showed his badge. The Special Branch officers backed off.

"Follow my lead, Sarah," Howard told her. "I still can't say I trust you."

The comment hurt Sarah, but she could find no fault in its reasoning. She had betrayed Howard, betrayed her country. She and the United Kingdom were in no way cosy companions, but she realised now that it was her home — love it or hate it — and right now it was under threat by her father.

They headed inside the Houses of Parliament and entered Confederation Hall. Immediately, they turned left towards the House of Commons. There were a pair of guards up ahead, sitting in ornately-wrought brass chairs either side of the entrance. Howard called out to them.

"Is Parliament still in session? Have you been fully briefed? Hey, stand up and answer me."

Sarah reached out and touched Howard's arm. "Howard..."

They approached the two Special Branch officers and Sarah noticed right away how their chins lay against their chests. Blood stained the top of their shirts and glistened.

Howard pulled out his gun. "Your father's already here. These men have no weapons."

Sarah stepped in front of Howard and kicked open the doors to the House of Commons, just as the first gunshot rang out. Chaos erupted throughout the tiered benches of the chamber. A flood of MPs tried to sprint towards the doors but many were mown down by automatic gunfire. They fell onto the stomachs, side by side, and formed a carpet of bodies. The remaining MPs, still well over a hundred in total, froze in place, cowering behind benches or lying completely flat on the floor. The Leader of the Opposition tried to stand tall and approach Major Stone, who stood on the Speaker's dais like a towering judge, but Prime Minister Breslow swatted the sallow man aside like a fly. She would be the one to deal with this situation, that much was clear.

Sarah's father spotted her presence and seemed surprised. "Sarah? Be a good daughter and close those doors, would you? I would hate to have to shoot anybody else."

Sarah played along and shoved the doors closed behind her and Howard. Howard had his gun levelled at her father, but it would be little match for the twin MP5s that the other man wielded. Krenshaw's briefcase lay on a table in front of Major Stone on the table in front of the Speaker's chair. He patted it and smiled.

Breslow turned on Sarah and glared. "I know you."

Sarah nodded. "My face is kind of hard to forget."

"You stopped Hesbani."

"I did."

"So why this? Why are you doing this?"

Sarah shook her head. "I'm not here to help my father. I'm here to stop him."

Breslow gave a cat-like grin and turned around to face Major Stone. "Least you raised a decent daughter, Major Stone."

Major Stone was unsmiling. "You know of me, Prime Minister?"

"I was briefed about what happened at Heathrow and warned that you may have been en route here. Bravo on gaining entry, Major. I believed the place quite fortified."

"It'll take more than a few upper-echelon civilians to stop me. If Special Branch is all you have to protect you, it's a miracle you've lived this long."

Breslow continued to smile. "You wouldn't be the first man to underestimate me, Major."

"I'll be the first to kill you, though. A woman has no place running the world of men. What could you understand of war and politics? Women exist to raise men, not dominate them. You are an abomination."

Breslow seemed unfazed by both the blatant misogyny and the pair of sub-machine guns aimed at her face. "What do you want, Major? You have just killed the Foreign Secretary and three members of the shadow cabinet. Despite what one might think, I considered them all friends."

Major Stone waved an arm around the room, making various MPs flinch as the MP5's crosshairs fell over them. "What I want is what you see: the submission of this malignant hive of malefactors followed by its complete annihilation."

Breslow nodded at the two MP5s he was holding. "Do you have enough bullets?"

He tapped the briefcase in front of him. "I have something better."

Howard took a step forward, gun still held up and aimed forward. "Prime Minister, MCU believes that the contents of that briefcase contain a deadly disease engineered by the man responsible of Ebola Reading."

Breslow looked at him. "That would be Dr Krenshaw, correct? Deceased?"

Howard nodded. "You've been well briefed."

"It pays to be, although it would seem one can never be too prepared." She turned back to Major Stone. "So, I return to my previous question: what do you want? If it is merely to kill us all then what's keeping you?"

Sarah felt a twinge of satisfaction as she watched the uncertainty cross her father's face. He obviously hadn't expected such brazenness from the Prime Minister, a woman. He gathered a hold of himself quickly, though, and gave the PM a glare so fiery that it would not have been surprising if she caught fire.

"I want the right-honourable peers assembled here to witness you admit your crimes. The people in this country need to see that our leader is no nobler than Saddam Hussain or Colonel Gaddafi were. I want to see you humbled to the lowly scorpion that you are — you and all those like you."

Breslow actually yawned then. The assembled MPs had crept out from their hiding places and were now enraptured by what they were seeing.

"So that's it," said Breslow. "You're just another disgruntled vet with a grudge against the men and women who commanded them? Did I ever give you an order, Major Stone? You'll have to forgive me for not remembering."

Major Stone spoke slowly. "Syria, September 13th, 2012."

Breslow looked at him blankly.

"There is the problem," he said in a voice more a growl than speech. "On that date, one-hundred-and-twelve innocent people lost their lives on your orders and you don't even remember. You have forgotten the bomb you dropped after I lased a target I was assured was a rebel outpost. But it wasn't, was it? You had me and my men light up a goddamn orphanage just to get one man, who wasn't even there. You wanted Al Al-Sharir so bad that you were willing to kill one-hundred children just to get him."

"You don't strike me as a man who values children, Major Stone."

"That's where you're wrong, Prime Minister. I care very much for children, for they are the only truly innocent of this world. They know nothing of bloodshed and greed, religion or politics. I even had a child myself, once. I tried to be a father for a while, was even pretty good at it. I would hold this child of mine on my lap, each night before putting her down to bed, and sing songs to her. Her beautiful little face would light up and something inside of me would light up, too. That beautiful face no longer exists, just another thing turned to scars and ashes by this damned nation."

Sarah brought her fingers to the scars on her face and suddenly felt weak. It was strange, but some ethereal feeling came over her where she could almost remember what her father was describing. She had brief snatches of sitting on a man's lap and feeling sleepy as the words of a lullaby soothed her. But as soon as the memory came it vanished. For that split-second she had had a loving father, and it had felt good.

Breslow took the floor again. "If the Intel was wrong, then it was your job to report it, Major."

Major Stone lifted his chin, staring down his nose at her. "I did report it. I saw the children thirty-seconds after I lased the building. I tried to call off the strike, but word came from above that my objections were received but overruled. Somebody high up felt that taking out Al-Sharir was important enough to drop the bomb anyway, collateral damaged be damned. That order came from you, Prime Minister."

Breslow huffed. "How could you possibly come to that conclusion? I have no hand in military operations other than sanctioning them."

"I am Major Stone. The men and women of the Armed Forces fear and respect me. I knew within the hour who gave the order. Men I would trust with my life swore that it came from the very top. Number 10 gave the order to continue with the bombing, despite the presence of over a hundred non-combatants. You killed a hundred children, Breslow. No, you have probably killed thousands since you came to power. You are a butcher. Now I will repay you for your sins."

Major Stone reached for the briefcase.

Sarah stepped forward. "Major Stone, stop!"

-22-

Her father looked at her. "I need to do this, Sarah. It's time that the right people were finally made to pay, instead of more innocents."

"There are people in this room who are innocent," said Sarah.

"Ha! Do you really believe that?"

She glanced around the room, at the frightened faces of the male and female MPs. All of them wore fine suits and seemed only concerned for themselves. "Perhaps not," she admitted, "but you open that briefcase and the virus kills a lot more people than are in this room. You were going to release it at Heathrow for Christ's sake. It's madness."

For the first time in her life, her father seemed insecure. His voice lost a measure of its authority and his glaring eyes failed to keep still. "Something has to change. Releasing the virus at the airport would have rocked the foundations of the earth. There are a group of powerful men ready to rebuild a better world, but first this one has to tumble."

"You sound insane," she said.

"Not insane, just exhausted. Say what you want about me, Sarah, but I have never done anything in anger or for revenge. Every bad deed I have ever done I have done with a clear head and a sense of duty. I'd never even felt rage until after what I saw them do to that orphanage, and what they did to you."

Sarah pointed to her scars and said angrily, "Hesbani did this to me and I killed him myself. I don't need anyone to feel angry on my behalf."

"A father has no choice, and not everybody is able to earn their own justice. You are one of the lucky ones, Sarah. All that the other victims of this country's militaristic greed have is me. I will bring them their justice."

Sarah headed away from the doors and towards her father at the Speaker's dais, ignoring Howard's warning to stay back. She stood before the Speaker's chair and looked up at her father. "Killing doesn't erase killing. This isn't what you devoted your life to. In the past, you took orders, but now you're making your own decisions, which means that all of this is on you."

Her father smiled at her, then actually began chuckling. It was a sad laugh, one that came before an emotional rupture. "I admit it," he said. "You make me proud, Sarah. That's what you want to hear, isn't it? I've always been proud of you. Somebody tells you that you can't do something and you set out to prove them wrong. The SAS is just the same. I, too, spent my life doing things that other men told me were impossible. You are a lot like me, Sarah. I just wish you'd been a man. Think of what you might have achieved then. Maybe we might have truly served alongside one another. Maybe then you would not be opposing me. It is a shame."

Howard stepped up beside Sarah and lowered his gun. "Major Stone, you have served this country with honour. Don't end your career this way."

"You think history will look upon me poorly?"

"Of course."

"Guy Fawkes once tried to destroy parliament and he is remembered as a beloved martyr. I feel, in time, I will be no different, but if not, I don't care. All I care about is Breslow admitting to her crimes. If she doesn't, I will release this virus and kill everyone in this room. There is no vanquishing the beast inside this box."

Breslow folded her arms. "I have nothing to admit to but doing my duty. My obligation is to the prosperity and welfare of this nation. Every time a country imperils us it imperils itself. The blood of those Syrian orphans is on Syrian hands."

All of the MPs in the room swallowed and grew pale. No doubt they wanted to see Breslow fall on her sword so that this could be over with, but Breslow did not bow down to terrorists.

"I admire men like you," said Breslow. "You do as you see fit, and there is no shame in that, but the problem is that you're a man. You lack any sort of finesse. Like a bull you charge at the red flag and hope to gore it with your horns. You see, a woman does not charge the red flag, she holds it so that men like you can chase it blindly until you are too tired to stand. If you had been a woman, Major Stone, you might have actual been of some use."

Major Stone's face went as red as the hypothetical red flag and he raised both MP5s at Breslow. The leader reacted quickly, running and diving behind one of the benches, managing somehow to keep hold of her heels. Left, standing out in the open, was the leader of the opposition. The gangly man took the full brunt of the dual machine gun fire. His dark, sunken eyes bulged from his head and his slanted teeth turned red as blood shot from his throat. He slumped forwards onto the centre table and knocked the mace onto the floor, the ceremonial staff needed to pronounce the House in session. Sarah watched it roll along the floor at her feet and settle in a puddle of blood.

Howard aimed and took a shot at Major Stone, but missed. Major Stone returned fire and sent Howard into cover. More MPs made for the doors but were quickly gunned down. Their bodies fell and blocked the doors from being opened. Sarah stood in the middle of the flying bullets and screaming MPs and kept her eyes on her father. He had placed the briefcase down on the Speaker's desk as he wielded an MP5 in each hand. He was choosing his shots carefully, picking off the most senior members of the House with single, precise rounds. The Education Secretary lay on her back, clutching her throat and making strangling sounds. Most of the ruling cabinet were dead and a good portion of the opposition, too.

Sarah raced forwards, leaping up onto the centre table and heading towards the raised Speaker's dais at the far end, where she leapt into the air. Her father was distracted, shooting the panicked MPs whilst also keeping one eye on Howard, the only other armed man in the room. Sarah made it onto the Speaker's dais and snatched at the briefcase, grabbing it with both hands. Major Stone immediately turned both guns on her, but didn't fire. Instead he shouted, "Sarah, no!"

Sarah landed back on the floor and immediately started running.

Howard leapt up and fired, suppressing Major Stone from retaliating. Sarah made it all the way back to the doors, where she proceeded to try and drag the bodies out of the way.

"Sarah, is that you?" It was Mattock. His strike team had arrived outside in the hallway.

"Yes, it's me. The doors are blocked. My father has killed half of parliament."

"That sodding nutter. Is it over? Do you have him?"

"No, I-"

"SARAH!"

Sarah flinched, spun around, looked for her father at the dais but did not see him.

Howard was hiding in the benches of the sitting government and he nodded over to the opposite side of the room when her eyes fell on him. On the opposite side of the chamber, her father had an arm wrapped around Breslow's neck and held an MP5 to her temple. The other MPs were huddled in a group nearby.

"Put down the briefcase," he demanded. "I will not be stopped."

Sarah made eye-contact with Breslow, who seemed entirely calm despite her predicament. The huddled MPs beside her were clutching their chests and breathing heavily.

"Just go," shouted Breslow. "Get that briefcase somewhere where it can't hurt anybody."

Sarah nodded and turned back towards the doors. Mattock and his men had taken to barging it and there was a slight opening now that was growing ever wider.

"The briefcase will open as soon as the timer runs out, Sarah," her father warned, his confident voice returned, "unless I put in the code. Put it down and get away from it." He sounded almost concerned.

"This bitch is going to admit to her crimes or the whole of London is going to start bleeding from their eye sockets by nightfall."

For the first time since this whole thing began, Sarah saw fear in Breslow's eyes.

"You were always going to release the virus, weren't you?" said Sarah.

"Of course. Killing the Government isn't enough, but with no one running the country the virus will be unstoppable. The United Kingdom will become a worldwide charity case. Eventually, the virus will spread worldwide, the population will diminish and the world will start over, better."

Sarah couldn't believe what she was hearing. "You want the apocalypse? What if this virus wipes out the planet?"

"Krenshaw designed the virus to infect only one out of every two people. At its worst it would merely kill half the world's population, and that's nothing but a good thing."

"No virus would be able to spread unopposed," said Breslow. "We'll fight it, we'll understand it, and we'll win. You cannot hope to change anything."

Sarah heard a whisper behind her and glanced back to see Mattock's face at the door. He was poking something through the gap at her. She took it at once and quickly slid it under her shirt and into the waistband of her trousers. Her father was staring at her but hadn't seemed to have notice the exchange.

"I need you to get away from here, Sarah. That briefcase is going to open whether you like it or not. I never did much for you, but I'm giving you the chance to save yourself."

"I already have a containment unit on the way," said Howard. "We'll secure the briefcase and dispose of it. It's over, Major Stone."

"Is it? I've lost track of time. The virus could be released in the very next minute. How quickly do you think your containment unit can get here?"

Howard swallowed so loud that it echoed in the chamber.

"Give me Breslow and I'll leave," said Sarah. "You want to save me then let all of these people go and I will get far away from here."

"Sarah, I'm not negotiating."

Breslow sniggered. "How novel. A terrorist refusing to negotiate with us."

Major Stone growled and let off a shot into the crowd, hitting an anonymous MP in the face. That was the last straw. The group of MPs bolted, leaping over benches and chairs, trampling one another and throwing each other aside in a bid to get to the doors. At that same moment, Mattock's team forced their way through the doors and began gathering the MPs to safety. Howard leapt from cover and joined Sarah in the middle of the chamber by the main table. "It's finished, Sarah. I understand if you want to get out of here."

She shook her head. "No, it's not over."

Major Stone still held the muzzle of an MP5 to Breslow's head. "You want the PM, then hand over the briefcase."

"Why?" asked Sarah. "If it's set to go off, then why do you even want it?"

"To make sure it goes off."

"You'll get sick, too. Is that how you want to die? Of a disease?"

"It's nobler than most the deaths I have seen."

"Okay," said Sarah. "I'll give you the briefcase and you give me the Prime Minister."

For once, Breslow kept her mouth shut. The horror had finally broken her resolve and she wore the vacant stare of a frightened hostage.

Her father nodded. "I'll meet you in the middle. I want your man to toss his gun aside."

Howard shook his head. "This isn't happening. You're not getting the briefcase and I am not disarming."

Sarah moved close to Howard and spoke into his ear. "It's okay. He won't shoot me. Mattock passed me a gun. Play along and I'll end this."

Howard looked uneasy, but he threw aside his gun. "Fine, but the moment you try to leave this building, Major, they're going to take you out."

"I'm ready to meet my end. Just hurry this up."

Sarah headed into the middle of the room and waited for her father to meet her.

-23-

Winter, 1984

"Hush now, sweetheart, it's time to go to sleep."

Five-year old Sarah fought to keep her eyes open, because she knew that once they closed she would fall asleep and her daddy would leave. Soon he would be leaving for work and she was going to miss him. How would she fall asleep without him there each night? How could she sleep without hearing him sing to her?

"It's okay to close your eyes, Sarah. I won't be leaving for a few more days and then I will be back home again before you know it. They're sending me to a place called Iraq where it's really sunny and there's lots of sand. I'm part of a very special team that will keep me safe and bring me home to you and your mum. You don't need to worry. You are my angel. The best thing in my entire life, but I have to go away to work so that I can give you everything you need. Just be a good girl and go to sleep and tomorrow we can go and feed the ducks at the pond."

Sarah yawned, but continued to keep her eyes open. Her daddy was the strongest and bravest daddy of them all, and she didn't want him to go. But right now she was so tired.

"Sing to me, daddy."

Her father kissed her forehead. "Of course. Lullaby and good night, with roses bedight

With lilies o'er spread is baby's wee bed..."

Five-year-old Sarah was asleep before she knew it.

Her father was gone the next day, his unit leaving earlier than expected. When he came back, he was never the same.

-24-

Major Stone stepped out from around the Speaker's dais, dragging the Prime Minister with him. She went willingly, apparently eager to exchange her life for something that might well end it anyway.

"It's your last chance to stop this, dad."

Major Stone looked at his daughter and grunted. "You can't stop a bullet once it's been fired."

Sarah sighed and lifted up the briefcase with one hand. With the other she reached behind her back and gripped the handgun Mattock had given her.

"Hand Breslow over."

"First, place the briefcase on the ground."

Sarah exhaled, wondering if she had the ability to do what she needed to do. She knelt down, placing the briefcase on the ground, and then remained in a crouch, gripping the gun behind her back and willing herself to spring up and unload a bullet into her father's face while she had the chance.

"You probably think I won't shoot you," her father said. "Even when you pull that gun you have. Wrong"

Sarah raised an eyebrow and managed to utter one word. "What?"

Her father levelled the MP5 at her and pulled the trigger.

Sarah's vision curled inwards and spun. She hit her head on the floor and was aware of nothing but her pulse beating in her temples. She looked to her side and saw Howard running towards her father, but he was shot before getting anywhere close. He pin wheeled around and disappeared behind the first row of benches.

Major Stone looked down at his daughter without sympathy. "I really am proud of you," he said, "but better men than you have tried to take me down and failed."

Then he grabbed Breslow around the neck and began moving away with her, taking the briefcase with him and keeping the MP5 against his hostage's head.

Sarah lay on the floor bleeding while Howard moaned nearby. She heard Mattock shouting, but it eventually changed to an order for his men to back off. There was no chance the cockney sergeant would take a risk with both the briefcase and Breslow's life on the line. Major Stone was well protected, even with a dozen guns aimed at him.

Eventually, one of Mattock's men broke free and came to Sarah's aid. He checked her over with his gloved hands, looking for damage. "You're okay," he said. "You've taken a slug in the shoulder, but you'll be fine."

Sarah didn't feel fine. The pain in her upper body felt like her bones were being pressed. She had been wrong about her father – he would dare to shoot her, but not fatally it seemed. Howard was okay too and he recovered enough to come help her to his feet. His vest had taken the full impact of the slug, which had been fired at him from some distance, and he had only been winded. Thank God they had both heeded Mattock's earlier warning to wear vests.

"We have to get after him," said Sarah, wincing as she held onto her shoulder.

Howard nodded. "Hell yes, we do. This is Wilder," he nodded to the member of Mattock's strike team who had come to their aid. A young man with messy blonde hair and fuzzy stubble — the Milky Bar Kid all grown up. "Wilder, this is Sarah Stone. She's with us."

Wilder nodded. "Mattock is already in pursuit. Special Branch snipers have been on the roof for the last hour. Major Stone has no place to go. He can't escape."

"He doesn't want to escape," said Howard. "He's ready to die and wants to take the whole world with him."

Wilder nodded as if he understood. "Then I saw 'a new heaven and a new earth,' for the first heaven and the first earth had passed away, and there was no longer any sea."

Sarah stared at Wilder in confusion until Howard explained. "This is no time for bible quotes, Wilder. The Book of Revelations can wait for another day."

Wilder nodded. "Amen, brother."

They headed back out into the hallways, leaving behind bloody footprints and memories of carnage. Even if they managed to stop Major Stone, nothing would ever be the same. Today would be a bloody entry forever etched in the history books. The Parliamentary Massacre of 2015, committed by her father, Major Jonathan Stone, father of Captain Sarah Stone. Now, Sarah would be ostracised for her lineage as well as her face. Her father was a worse man than she had ever thought him to be. She would be doing the world a favour by being the one to place the full-stop on his life.

They headed out of the building and were met by a Police cordon held by countless officers keeping back the crowds. Blinking flash bulbs went off like disco lights, even in the bright afternoon sunlight. Her face would be on tomorrow's papers — the disfigured daughter of a traitor — but none of that mattered right now. If Krenshaw's virus got out, there would be far more for the papers to worry about than today's bloodshed.

Her father was walking through the crowd, pushing Breslow ahead of him, the briefcase held beside him. No one tried to stop him, for all the officers understood the risk of being the one to pull the trigger.

Wilder let out a whistle. "There must be a hundred fingers on triggers right now, but not a single one brave enough to pull."

"Nobody wants to be the one to miss and hit the PM," said Howard.

Sarah kept back, wanting to see what her father was planning. Was his plan only to ensure the briefcase opened? Was Breslow his insurance to ensure he lived long enough to see it? Was the virus really so infectious that it would spread regardless of where it was released?

Major Stone headed down the road slowly, moving his eyes in all direction and making no sudden movement that might prompt a deadly response.

"Let the PM go," Mattock bellowed from the front of one of the police units through a microphone.

Major Stone turned back to answer. "Sergeant Mattock, you should know most of all what I am fighting for. You've seen."

"Too right," he said. "And I much prefer it to watching innocent women and children dying. You knew the risks when you signed up. War is bloody, but we're working our way out of it. It's men like you and Hesbani who ensure we never get to wash our hands clean of blood."

Major Stone didn't allow himself to be distracted further and started moving faster along the road. He was heading in the direction of Westminster Bridge. The traffic had been halted at the far end and the road and on the opposite bank of the Thames. The way was completely clear. Sarah broke free of Howard and Wilder and headed after her father. The two men went after her, but kept a few feet back, not yet knowing what she planned to do.

Her father was almost in the centre of the bridge when she finally caught up to him, out of breath and still bleeding from the gunshot wound in her shoulder. Helicopters swirled overhead with the black silhouettes of snipers hanging from them. The tops of nearby buildings also sported the tell-tale flashes of long-range rifle scopes. Major Stone would be hit from a dozen directions if he let go of Breslow for a single second.

It had to happen here, Sarah decided, in the centre of the bridge where there were no innocent bystanders.

"Daddy, stop!"

Major Stone stopped and turned around, dragging Breslow along like a rag doll. "Don't force me to shoot you somewhere serious, Sarah. I may be many things, but I wouldn't like to be the type of man who kills his children. Tell your men to back off, too, or I'll execute the PM right here."

Howard and Wilder heard and kept their distance.

"You don't have to shoot me," said Sarah, "and I don't want you to. I just want this all to be over. I understand why you're doing this. I'm tired of the way things are, too. It's all wrong. The wrong people are getting hurt all the time, while the guilty get rich in safety. But don't you see the hypocrisy of this? I don't give two shits about Breslow, but if that virus gets out then a lot more children are going to die than in that Syrian orphanage. Have you even thought about that?"

"I've thought about nothing else, but they will die to ensure a better future."

Sarah tried to straighten up, but her wounded shoulder would not allow her. She settled for taking a knee and facing her father from lower down. "You sound like a fundamentalist," she said. "You sound like the type of men you used to hate."

"Perhaps I do. It's probably because I discovered they are just men and nothing more. That is the great lie the government sells to its public, Sarah. They make the other side seem like monsters, and believe me, some of them are, but many are no different to us. The only thing different is the colour of their skin and the word they use to describe God."

Sarah shook her head. "You're blind."

"My eyes have never been more open. Any moment now this briefcase will open and things will change forever. It's your last chance to get out of here."

"Give me Breslow and I will. There are snipers everywhere, dad. Giving up Breslow is the only way you get to walk away from this."

"I don't want to walk away from this." Her father shoved Breslow in the back, but not towards Sarah. He sent the woman toward the bridge's barrier, keeping his gun on her. There he ordered the PM to climb upwards and once she was perched precariously on the barrier, he vaulted up to join her. It had afforded the snipers the brief opportunity to shoot, but none had.

Major Stone put the MP5 to Breslow's temple and held the briefcase over the Thames with the other.

Sarah got up off her knee and took a step forward. "What are you doing?"

"Any sniper shoots me and the virus goes into the river, along with Breslow's brains. People will be drinking it all in their tea by nightfall."

"If I have my way," said Breslow, seeming to come out of her frightened stupor all of a sudden. "The snipers will leave you wounded so I can take you alive. Then I'll have you tortured and your head put on a spike over Tower Bridge."

Major Stone grunted. "How draconian. Use my head as a football for all I care, once this is over." He lowered his weapon for a second, and began fiddling with the briefcase's dial.

"I thought it was on a timer," said Sarah. "You were bluffing"

Major Stone clenched his jaw, still fiddling with the dial. "You thinking that this thing is set to blow is the only thing that has kept me alive. Don't worry, though. I'm about to open it right in the river."

Sarah made eye-contact with Breslow, who understood immediately. The PM clenched her hands together and swung them like a hammer into Major Stone's guts. He doubled over, more in shock than pain, but was distracted long enough that the Briefcase fell from his hands and clattered on the road. Breslow threw herself from the barrier, landing face-first on the hard surface of the road. "Shoot him," she screamed. "Shoot the sonofabitch."

Sarah raised her gun and aimed it at her father's chest, but she didn't pull the trigger — couldn't.

Major Stone smirked at her. "You just can't shoot your old man, can you?"

"Give up."

"Not in this lifetime." Major Stone pointed the MP5 at Breslow and pulled the trigger.

But not before Sarah had pulled hers.

The shot was close enough that the round went clear through Major Stone's chest and left him tottering on the barrier of the bridge. He looked at Sarah in shock, his lips sliding back and forth soundlessly, his eyes flickering. He placed a hand to his bleeding chest and then removed it to take a look at his blood. With a chuckle he then spoke to his daughter, "Well done, man. Well done indeed."

Then the snipers fired from a dozen direction and sent Major Stone's dancing body plummeting into the Thames where his body floated and went still.

There was no time to think before scores of men came running up the bridge from both banks. Howard and Mattock came and took a hold of Sarah first, making sure she didn't faint and that no one could take her away. But she was okay and waved them off.

"You just shot your old man," said Mattock, although he sounded more than a little supportive of the act.

"Are you okay?" Howard asked her.

"I'm fine." She stood back while a group of space-suited gentlemen scooped up the briefcase and placed it inside a plastic crate with great big seals that clamped down around the edges.

"Did the briefcase go off?" asked Howard. "Did it go off?"

Sarah shook her head. "He was bluffing. The timer was never set after we left the airport."

Mattock huffed. "If I'd know that, I'd have taken his bloody head off myself an hour ago."

"Yeah," Sarah said, walking over to the edge of the bridge and staring down at the water below. Her father's lifeless body was being dragged into a police boat like the rotting carcass of a seal. His illustrious career ended in ignominy.

Breslow approached her with a pained limp, rubbing dirt off her suit and combing stray strands of hair back behind her ears. "You've saved the day again, Miss Stone. Seems like I need to have you on speed dial."

Sarah didn't smile at the comment. Her expression was blank as she spoke. "The men from my past seem to have a habit of causing trouble and dragging me into it. If you had any sense you'd lock me up and throw away the key."

"Nonsense. This country needs women like you to put men in their place. In the House of Commons, I can hold my own, but it's good to know that when things get tough, there's a bitch as tough as me who knows how to use a gun."

Sarah looked down at the gun in her hands and found it to be an ugly thing. "Half of Parliament is dead."

"Yes," said Breslow, followed by another, more thoughtful, "Yes."

The PM was eventually ferreted away by her frantic servants, so Sarah went on over to Howard. She held her wrists out in front of her and said, "I'm ready to face the music. I was part of this."

Howard took her gun from her and placed it into his belt. Then he pulled a pair of handcuffs from under his suit jacket and held them over her wrists, but then he hesitated.

"What are you waiting for?"

He sniffed and put the cuffs away. "As I see it, the only crime you're guilty of is shooting a member of the MCU." He turned to Mattock who merely shrugged.

"I don't hold grudges," he said. "Just buy me a couple beers and we'll call it even."

Sarah chuckled. "How about a dozen?"

"Then it's decided," said Howard.

"You're letting me go?"

"No way. After all this, your arse belongs to me. You want forgiveness, then you can damn well earn it. You're joining the MCU — permanently, this time."

Sarah didn't even need to think about it. She knew where she belonged. "If the MCU can put up with my ugly mug, then there's no place I'd rather be."

Howard surprised her then by grabbing her shoulder and pulling her in for a hug. "We missed you."

Mattock made them both laugh by murmuring the word, "Hippies."

It was all over, and for the first time in perhaps her entire life, Sarah felt wanted. She held Howard in the hug long enough for him to eventually drag himself free. "You've changed," he said with a frown. "You weren't really the cuddly type when we first met."

Sarah smiled. "You have no idea how much I've missed you guys. Never let me get kidnapped by a deranged madman ever again, okay?"

"No promises."

-25-

Mattock took Wilder and re-joined the strike team outside the Houses of Parliament, while Howard and Sarah met up with Mandy and headed back to MCU headquarters on the outskirts of High Wycombe. The Earthworm had been half abandoned when Sarah had first visited it and had been in rubble by the time she left, but Howard assured her that the place had changed a great deal in the last six months. MCU's recent successes had brought an influx of government spending and they were now close to being fully staffed. Their location was still secret, despite the MCU now being a household name in UK law enforcement.

Mandy took the Range Rover off the main road and onto a field where a ten-minute bumpy ride led to a derelict farm. When she saw the big old barn, Sarah knew she was home. She got out of the car with Howard, while Mandy stayed inside and parked inside the cover of the old barn.

The secret hatch inside the old shed opened upon Sarah and Howard's arrival and she allowed him to lead her down the long staircase into the earth. At the bottom they reached the first inner hatch and stepped through into a room she no longer recognised.

The Earthworm's tail section was alive, unlike the previously dead and dusty space she had visited. The previously abandoned space, the size of a football pitch, was now staffed with dozens of young men and women, all of them typing at computers or chattering into headsets. Everyone was so busy that not a single one noticed Howard and Sarah's arrival and they were free to walk right through the centre of the room.

"Told you things had changed," said Howard. "We have several dozen analysts working here now and Mattock has been moved to the senior team along with Jessica, Palu, and me. We have a new guy coming soon from the D.C. office to help us coordinate with US operations. I'm afraid Jessica has gone a little too native to be considered a liaison anymore."

Sarah chuckled. Her relationship with Dr Jessica Bennett had been strained to begin with, two independent women rarely got along easily, but towards the end they had begun to see eye to eye and had even began approaching the fringes of a friendship. "Is Palu expecting me?" she asked.

"Yes, I called ahead. He was happy to hear we hadn't lost you to the other side. Things looked a little hairy, there, for a while. We thought your father had brainwashed you."

"He did. I was completely lost, even before my father kidnapped me, but now I finally know who I am. This is where I want to be."

Howard nodded. "Good."

They headed through the Earthworm's middle section, which had been a smoking ruin not six months ago, and headed straight for the head section. There, Howard used his thumbprint to open the hatch and they stepped through into the MCU command centre. Palu and Jessica sat there, waiting expectantly. They stood up when they saw her.

"Captain Stone," said Jessica in an accent far less American than Sarah remembered. "Glad to have you back with us."

"I'm glad to be back, and no 'Captain,' please. I'm just a new recruit now."

Palu smiled. He seemed smaller and wearier than she remembered, but the glint in his eyes was vibrant and alive. "You're anything but a recruit, Sarah. Taking down your father can't have been easy. Are you okay?"

Sarah prodded the scars on her face and said, "I have a lot of demons in my past, but my daddy was the worst of them all. If I dealt with him, I can deal with anyone. Yeah, I'm okay. I'm actually feeling kind of good, in a way."

Howard patted her on the back. "Take a seat, Sarah. We can do the debriefing now and then get some sleep in the dorms. They'll be more bad guys to fight tomorrow."

Sarah took the seat. "I just hope the next villain I have to take down is outside of my family."

"Before we begin," said Palu. "I need to introduce you and Howard to our new Intelligence Officer. He arrived an hour ago, having travelled from MCU's newly formed D.C. branch. I'll just give him a buzz and bring him in."

Howard took a seat next to Sarah and looked at Jessica. "What's the new guy like?"

"Handsome."

Sarah laughed. "Are you on the market, Dr Bennett?"

Jessica chuckled. "A single lady is always on the market for the right man."

One of the room's side doors opened and a tall man stepped into the command centre. Everyone stood up to greet him, but Sarah did so more quickly than the others. In fact, she leapt to her feet in shock.

"Thomas?"

Thomas stepped further into the room and smiled at her. "Hello, Sarah. I've missed you."

Howard glanced at Sarah. "You know this man?"

She nodded her head slowly. "Yes, he's my dead husband."

-27-

It had been a long and tiring wait. Heathrow had remained on lockdown for forty-eight hours, which made the delay in Moscow almost unbearable. But he was a patient man and had been waiting for far longer than two days for the journey he was finally undertaking. His imminent plans had been ten years in the making and a delayed flight was inconsequential as a result.

The Russian envoy stepped out of the airport and stretched their legs on the pavement, taking in great lungful's of crisp British air. It was a glorious day, made even more glorious by their arrival. The city of London had been cowed, its hubris dismantled, first by Hesbani and then by one of its own soldiers turned rogue. The United Kingdom no longer trusted in its safety and there were scant few politicians left alive to provide the public the succour it needed. The rumours of a great, man-made disease currently being held at a Porton Down laboratory gave the nation nightmares and even the confident bluster of Prime Minister Breslow was not enough to give the country back its spine. The United Kingdom was no longer united. It was crumbling into dust. And very soon, it would be finished.

Yuri was smiling happily. The Russian diplomat had visited the UK many times in the past and often spoke of his fondness for it. Peter was little different and wasted no time in ordering a Cornish pasty from a nearby vendor. It was disrespectful to love a nation more than one's own and the two Russian diplomats were sickening in their display of affection for the country that was, in many ways, their enemy. It was no secret that Moscow despised the West as much as any Middle Eastern state, but its seat in the global assembly was precarious and came with shackles. As much as Moscow needed to play nice on the world stage, it was only a means to an end. There were more ways to topple the West than by flying Planes into buildings or battling over isolated oil reserves.

A sleek black limousine awaited the three men outside the terminal and Peter and Yuri hurried excitedly towards it, further sickening the stomach of their silent companion. At least the man who greeted them was a true Russian. Vladimir Rusev was a portly man with a harsh face that never smiled. Yet, when he spotted the three men leaving the airport he greeted them warmly. "Peter," he said, shaking hands. "Yuri. How are things in Moscow? Glorious I hope. And you, my good friend, it has been too long."

Al Al-Sharir smiled. "Yes," he said. "Indeed it has. But now that I am here, Vladimir, I expect things to move along very quickly."

Rusev nodded and winked. "Very quickly indeed, my friend. Everything you need is in place. We have been waiting for you. Welcome to the United Kingdom."

"Thank you," said Al Al-Sharir. "I came just in time to see it fall."

END.

Book 3 Coming Soon

About The Author

Iain Rob Wright is one of the UK's most successful horror and suspense writers, with novels including the critically acclaimed, THE FINAL WINTER; the disturbing bestseller, ASBO; and the wicked screamfest, THE HOUSEMATES.

His work is currently being adapted for graphic novels, audio books, and foreign audiences. He is an active member of the Horror Writer Association and a massive animal lover.

Check out Iain's official website or add him on Facebook where he would love to meet you.

www.iainrobwright.com
FEAR ON EVERY PAGE